Enjoy these **PRIMROSE U.S.M.C.** titles from
R. Michael Haigwood

First Tour - Rescue
Second Tour - Suitcase
Third Tour - Sleeper Cell
Finders Keepers

The cover shows the USS Hornet (CVA-12) underway
off the cost of North Vietnam, September 1967.

PRIMROSE U.S.M.C.

Third Tour - Sleeper Cell

R. Michael Haigwood

CONTENTS

Thanks to those who gave inspiration for the characters:

Robert J. Nakonieczny, USMC

Michael J. Nakonieczny, USMC

Thomas P. (Maddog) Naughton, USMC

H. C. Bowden, USMC

T. J. Martinez, .USMC

Two Case Chapman, USMC

Harold Davidson, USN

Larry Hauder , USN

Mac McKenzie, USN

Gary Kruegar, USN

W D. (Butch) Schroder, USA

R. P. Sullivan, USA

John La Mont, USA.

Ronni Sullivan, Civilian

Jerry McElligott, Civilian

Gus (Sweet Freddie) Fuson, American Indian

Acta non verba!

CHAPTER 1

I-Corps, Third Marine Division,
Third Battalion, Scout Sniper Platoon,
Vietnam

The young corporal entered Lieutenant Primrose's tent and announced, "Lieutenant Primrose, Lieutenant Colonel Easy wants to see you, and he seems a little agitated. As a matter of fact, I think I'll go to chow while the lieutenant is in with the colonel. If I were the lieutenant, I would hustle my ass right over there. Excuse my frankness, sir."

Lieutenant Primrose responded to the brash corporal, "Corporal, get your butt over to chow before I take you with me to see the commanding officer."

"Yes sir, I'm on my way."

Lieutenant Primrose had taken a battlefield commission after a couple of highly successful missions on his last tour, and Colonel Easy was a good friend, but still his commanding officer and the two don't mix on duty.

Primrose was thinking on his way over to Easy's tent, *I wonder what the fuck I did now! I don't think I like this lieutenant shit, with every Tom, Dick, and Harry on your ass for something or another. I don't see anything I've done recently to warrant an ass chewing. Maybe one of my Marines has his butt in a sling—that must be it! I'll go to the wall for every one of them—*

no matter what. Guess I better get my ass over to his unconventional company office, and in the meantime rethink this promotion shit.

Primrose reported in to the colonel, "Zachary Taylor Primrose, Lieutenant of Marines, reporting as ordered, sir."

The colonel was sitting at his makeshift desk, when he looked up at the sound of the door jamb being hammered. The source of the noise was the best lieutenant he'd ever commanded. He waved the five-ten, one-eighty, brown-haired Marine with green eyes into his quarters/office, glad he'd recommended him for a commission. "Cut the shit, Lieutenant Primrose. You're lucky I don't have you drawn, quartered, and reduced to PFC. You've certainly done everything in your power to warrant a decommissioning ceremony."

Lieutenant Colonel Easy had been in command of Primrose since he arrived in-country. They were on their second tour, with number three in the immediate future. He continued to address the newly promoted Lieutenant. "Your request for another tour has been denied by the Commandant of the Marine Corps. They think two tours is enough, and I imagine your wife, Rhonda, has the same feelings. On the other hand, I suppose with her working in Bangkok, it's better than her being in the real world; at least you can get together once in a while. But I didn't call you up here to discuss your domestic affairs. There is another matter that needs your full, undivided attention."

It was time for Primrose to step up to the plate and protect his troops, "Who was it, sir?"

"Who was what? What the hell are you talking about?"

"Sir, I was under the impression that one of my guys had fucked up, and that's why I'm here."

A slight smile crossed the colonel's face as he remembered their last mission. "Yes, Lieutenant, come to think of it, that's exactly why you're here. It's not one of your guys, but three of your retarded friends. The names you'll recall, I'm sure. O, McPotts, and Ourdae. Do you remember those three troopers, Lieutenant?"

The three names brought Primrose good memories of a mission they'd had on the Mekong river, a mission that had given him his recent rank. Colonel Easy's promotion resulted from the same operation.

"Yes sir, I do remember. Brave and loyal men of the first order. But sir, the last that was heard of the trio is that they were KIA somewhere in the Mekong Delta."

The colonel was nearly laughing out loud at the false sincerity of Primrose. He turned around in his chair to keep Primrose from seeing the humor on his face and blowing his persona of mean and nasty.

"Lieutenant, let's eliminate all the crap. There is a WWII PT boat missing in the delta, with two missing sailors and one misguided Marine on board running all over the fucking Mekong Delta causing destruction and mayhem. Have they been resurrected from the dead? I'll venture to say the PT and its motley crew haven't strayed far from the area of our last mission, and I would also speculate that you have contacted or could contact the aforementioned crew. How am I doing so far? I know you and those rogues were closer than two coats of paint. I told the brass up at Division that very thing.

"Division has been on my ass for information on those three ever since the PT boat—now known as the 'Ghost Boat,' by the way—started creating havoc. Everyone has to admit they've done more good than harm, but they keep stealing government property and harassing some very important people on our side, not just the enemy."

Primrose stood at attention and listened to the colonel with a slight smile, knowing his pals were particularly good at creating havoc.

"The shit story that stealing government property is really just moving it from one location to another without orders or requisitions won't fly, but the brass says due to their being on the plus side of things, mainly enemy dead, they've decided to give them a break."

Primrose had to show a sober face as he responded to Easy. "I agree, sir, they are deserving, if they are still alive."

The three rogues had gone AWOL after the last mission the colonel led and had been fighting the enemy on their terms, not wanting or liking the military rules of engagement. The river and delta had become their personal battleground. O, was an experienced brown water sailor (brown water means river), who had been a friend of McPotts, the former Navy navigator who had left the Navy for the Marine Corps, and Ourdae was a Corpsman with the experience of any combat gritty Marine. They all had suspect service record books and were not fondly thought of in the higher echelons of either service, but to their fellow grunts or sailors they were the best.

Col. Easy had to admire Primrose for his leadership qualities and his good sense to hide his admiration for the three clowns on the river. "Zip it up and listen, Lieutenant. You're not fooling me about their breathing or not, okay?"

"Yes sir."

"Primrose, if those shitbirds will come in with the PT boat at a certain location on a given date, the brass will have them reinstated as active duty recovered POW's—with all rank, privileges, back pay, and awards due them, and their SRB's wiped clean."

Lieutenant Primrose, gave the colonel a questioning look. "What's the catch, sir?"

"Primrose, it sounds like you don't have any faith in the good judgement of the Marine Corps."

"Sir, we're at war, and there are always strings attached to any dangling bait."

Colonel Easy pondered the look on Primrose's face, and decided to just come out with what Division had given him. "Yes, well, there are a couple of things that need attention, which will require some risk to life and limb to make all the other good things come to pass."

"Sir, is this some kind of *special*, special mission?"

"No shit, Primrose, and if you want to lead them, you'll be able to extend your tour. Division knows you know where they are and how to contact them. Division has been biding their time, waiting for the right situation to use their special talents. So do you want in?"

"Damn," Primrose thought.

"Sir, if I can extend my tour, it sounds good to me. Rhonda is working in Bangkok with her all-girl, round-eye band, and it's going great guns. Those little brown fuckers really like the round-eyes stuff. If we can stay another year, our combined income will put us in good shape when we head back to the real world. With her traveling between Phnom Penh, Hong Kong, Bangkok, and Taiwan, we don't see much of each other anyway—so yes, I'm in. What's the next step?"

The colonel was sure the addition of the lieutenant would put the operation on solid footing. His connections would enhance their chances for success, and besides the guy was turning out to be a damned good leader of Marines.

"Your next step is to rein in the PT with its rogue crew and stand by for orders. We'll discuss their pay, awards, and so on at a later date; this mission can't wait for all the formalities. I'll go into detail on the operation with you after I receive my marching orders. I'm flying out to a carrier on Yankee Station for the operational briefing. This affair is top secret, and I mean that in the strictest sense of the word."

"Yes sir."

"Now get to work on finding your motley crew, and have them ready to mount out with little or no notice!"

Because of the past history of the PT and its crew, the colonel thought they would be the best bet for what he knew of the mission so far. Finding them wouldn't be a problem for Primrose, as Rhonda was in constant contact with the three river pirates. The deal Division was offering would be hard to turn down, and he, along with Primrose, were hoping the crew was ready to take advantage of a great opportunity to get their life back in the event they wanted to head home to the world again.

O would be the odd man out, but McPotts and Ourdae would surely take the offer, not being brown water sailors from the beginning like O.

CHAPTER 2

South Vietnam off Yankee Station,
Carrier *Hornet*

Colonel Easy could hear the pilot through the headset yelling, "Hang on, Colonel, it's going to be a little rough when we touch the deck."

Easy always thought a chopper landing on a carrier was pretty much like landing on the tarmac at any airfield, although on this occasion the deck looked like a sawhorse teeter-totter on a playground, with the carrier diving in and popping out of the swells. The landing was almost as exciting as coming into a hot LZ with everyone on the planet shooting at the chopper. The door gunner was smiling at the colonel with that smile someone gets when they're enjoying your misery.

They bounced a couple of times and then settled down. He felt hands throwing him out of the hatch, into the arms of the flight deck crew. They herded him over to the nearest portal, where a very large Marine pointed to the endless stairwells that led up to officer country. After an exhausting climb, he stumbled into the Special Operations Room, where he faced an officer whose rank got his attention as to how serious the mission was going to be.

He looked up to see a tall, thin, gray-haired Navy Captain standing behind a desk in the operations room. He felt his cold, black eyes penetrating him. Easy fumbled around, not expecting to see a full fledged captain. "Lieutenant Colonel Easy reporting as ordered, sir."

"Welcome aboard, Colonel. My name is Captain Shutes. I'm the briefing officer for the mission, which I might add is TOP SECRET!"

Easy didn't have any problem noticing if the captain had a sense of humor: he didn't. "How was the landing, Colonel, with the deck moving about like your grandmother's old Maytag washing machine?"

"Sir, I would prefer a stiff gunfight in the roughest jungle on the planet, compared to landing on your carrier in this turbulent weather."

The captain didn't smile, so Easy figured he was right in his first impression of him. The guy was dead-ass serious, and any attempts at humor were wasted.

The captain was nearly standing at attention when he began, "Let's get right to it, Colonel. I'll start the briefing, and others will fill in the blanks. The priority is red flag for this operation, a damned serious situation is in the works as we speak. First I'll bring you up to date from the birth of this flap. We're in day one of the unfolding events, and you need to be on the road by day two. I know this is short notice. We have some very good reports on you and your people. Something to the effect that your methods are, should we say, 'off center,' to say the least—this is exactly what is needed on this mission. You'll be working independent of all contact from our end: that includes the airways. The only communication that may be used in an extraordinary emergency situation is a landline. This will be a last resort: you should be on the verge of death. We'll work on that communication later, but first I'll explain what has gone down so far." The captain was looking straight at the Marine Lieutenant Colonel. What he saw was a ramrod straight man with a red handlebar mustache, pale blue eyes, about five-ten, one-seventy, with a slight snicker that appeared to be permanent, and self-confidence oozing from every pore. The Corps had chosen well.

"Captain, I can have my troops on the road and ready to shove off with eight hour's notice. Given the proper equipment and transportation, we can be a positive force anywhere you desire to deploy us."

The captain was pleased with the attitude of the Marine, and responded, "Colonel, when we finish here, you'll have everything you need—and I mean *everything*! That should give you a clue how important this flap is. The brass chose your team because of your experiences in Laos and Cambodia. And there was some talk that you fellows had something to do wilh liberating a few POWs and using some very special weapons and explosives."

"I lay no claim to that rumor sir."

"It was also noted that your people can make things disappear and do it very well."

Colonel Easy was getting tired of the Captain's probing, and said, "Sir, I have a few good men. We're at the peak of our game, and we're always looking forward to the next mission. I believe you people have made a good choice. I can assure you, sir, you can have the greatest confidence in our abilities, no matter the situation."

"Okay, Colonel Easy, you have convinced me. It goes like this: a couple of days ago, two F-4 Phantoms, with a full complement of arms aboard, took off from this carrier and when they reported feet dry, they disappeared below the radar screen. These two particular fast movers had the latest radar, up-to-the-minute guidance systems, and every electronic gadget known to man. They also were armed with the latest missiles and rockets. You name it, they were carrying it. Most of it was being carried for the first time into combat.

"Your mission will be to locate the two F-4s, bring back the bodies of the pilots and all the electronic hardware you can, and destroy the rest—everything, leave nothing but a grease spot in the jungle."

Easy wanted more information. "Sir, do we have any idea if the two went down together or are they miles apart?

"We're not sure about that Colonel, but we think closer rather than farther. We have some coordinates for you to start with."

The captain turned to the lieutenant standing next to the wall map. "Lieutenant, please point out the area on the map where the colonel will begin his search."

Using a long pointer, the captain's aide directed their attention to the area in question and said, "At their air speed, they probably went down in this blue region here, within a mile or two."

Lieutenant Colonel Easy turned to Captain Shutes and remarked, "Captain, when I first met with the Marine General about this operation, he gave me a very limited heads-up on this so I could begin getting personnel and equipment together. I have at my disposal a WWII PT boat; it may be just the ticket to find the crash site. We'll need air transport to Phnom Penh, where the boat is located."

"You'll have transportation at your disposal, just let them know where you desire to go. We have taken satellite photos of the whole area. Nothing came up. Those two would have had to make a pretty big splash when they hit the jungle deck. Something is amiss here, and we need to know what that is!"

"Captain, have the Marine detachments at the embassies in Bangkok and Phnom Penh been notified about any of this?"

"No, Colonel, they haven't. This affair is being kept very close to the vest, for obvious reasons."

"Captain, we need to go over this assistance thing again. There must be a way to contact the proper people if we get in a bind."

"You don't contact anybody in the military. If you can find assistance from some other source, be my guest. We won't be involved, because we can't authorize you to be there. From what I hear, you and your troops operate very well outside the reach of authority, so hanging out there on a limb shouldn't be a problem for you! You'll be given anything you need in the way of equipment, transportation, and so on, but no outside help with troops, aircraft, boats or anything else that could connect higher authority with your rogue adventure if you know what I mean!"

The colonel was perplexed about the whole situation. He'd never heard of an operation where the brass didn't want to hear anything about it after it was launched. The hair started to tingle on his neck. "Well then, Captain, how do I contact the Navy when we find the crash site and discover what happened?"

"You don't make contact. Just bring everything you can out with you, especially the electronics and guidance systems. The state of the art equipment can't fall into enemy hands. The pilots, as I said before, have to be recovered dead or alive. As you might suspect their heads are full of very important information.

"If they've been captured, you're to rescue them. Then we'll know what the hell happened, and the enemy won't have an opportunity to discover their pain threshold. The best we have don't just go down without a trace. There is a trail out there somewhere. I wish you well, Colonel. Please step into the outer office for your charts and orders."

Colonel Easy, was not pleased with the captain, being so vague, but cooperative at the same time. The whole thing seemed a little too convoluted.

CHAPTER 3

The Admiral

The hair on Colonel Easy's neck began to bristle, as from a cold wind blowing across a frozen lake. The Navy was being antagonistic one moment and cooperative the next. The captain was being typical when dealing with grunt-ass Marines: a superior attitude, patronizing smiles, and hand shakes. The meeting was becoming a little to much for Colonel Easy and he said, "How the hell can two Phantom F-4s come up missing, and why the night run with experimental stuff aboard? And the coordinates the lieutenant gave are in Cambodia. This whole affair has a smell to it!"

"It's time to get on with the program, Colonel."

Colonel Easy was dismissed in an offhand manner not to his liking.

Standing outside the captain's ready room, Easy thought, *Why the hell didn't they get some people to do this mission who were a lot closer and already on alert? Finding a couple of downed jets isn't brain surgery. Like the captain said, they should have left a huge signature where they went down.* There was a lot going on here that he hadn't been made privy to. So Easy did an about face and marched right back to the captain's ready room to get some answers.

When he rapped on the captain's hatch and announced he was back, the captain didn't sound surprised or happy. "Enter, Colonel Easy. What's on your mind?"

With the stern posture of a combat-savvy Marine, he said, "Captain, may I speak frankly for a moment?"

"Sure, Colonel, what can I do for you?"

Easy slowed down and remembered he was speaking to a superior officer. Toning his voice down to a civil level, he said, "Sir, I believe you should give me the whole story on this flap, because the one you just gave me is a crock of shit if I may I be so blunt, sir!"

The captain tried to appear nonchalant, but didn't succeed. "Colonel, I told the admiral you wouldn't buy the BS I just tried to sell you. He had planned to piecemeal information as events warranted. I suppose it should all be on the table upfront. Follow me, Colonel, and we'll visit the admiral."

The captain led Easy through the maze of stairwells up to the admiral's quarters. When they approached the admiral's passageway, a Marine corporal was on watch and inquired, "Good evening Captain, Colonel. May I help you?"

The corporal was all business, he was under arms, his uniform detailed to the tenth degree, and he would not hesitate to give up his life to protect the admiral.

His stern manner didn't please a Navy captain, who had to go through a corporal to see the admiral.

"Yes, Corporal. We would like to see the admiral."

"Yes sir. I don't see you on my list, sir."

"Please tell the Admiral I'm here with the Marine officer from the mainland. I'm sure he'll be okay with that."

The corporal was enjoying the word game with the captain. The corporal didn't seem to like the captain and was doing all he could to prod him. Colonel Easy was enjoying the scene, as he didn't like the captain either.

"Yes sir. I'll check with the admiral."

The corporal rapped on the admiral's hatch and opened it without waiting for an answer.

"Sir, Captain Shutes from special operations is here with a Marine lieutenant colonel."

A rough voice replied, "Send them in, Corporal."

"Yes sir. Gentlemen, the Admiral will see you now."

The Corporal opened the hatch all the way and stood at attention, a smile neatly disguised on his face.

The captain thanked the corporal and said, "After you, Colonel."

Colonel Easy felt like a sacrificial lamb as he entered the lion's den first, taking any flack coming their way from the admiral. His dislike for the captain became ingrained forever more.

"Good evening, Captain...Colonel; what can I do for you?"

"Admiral, Colonel. Easy would like to be brought up to speed from the beginning on our present situation."

The admiral was a puffy sort, a little overweight, with gray hair and gray, piercing eyes. He didn't smile as he brought Easy up to date. "Colonel, we were trying to piecemeal this thing out to keep it from getting legs. This is the most sensitive flap that has come up since we've been on Yankee Station. Those two F-4 Phantoms had experimental stuff aboard, as you probably learned from Capt. Shutes. Along with those things, there was a device to make them invisible to radar with the flip of a switch and a night vision thing that would make a mission seems like it was a daylight.

"I suppose you can understand the significance of those two little items! We could attack the surface-to-air-missile sites with impunity, the bombings being a complete surprise to the NVA. The North Vietnamese wouldn't know we were there until the bombs were dropping on them.

It is imperative that we find the F-4s, as the captain said. You are to bring everything back that's possible to recover and destroy the rest. I can't impress upon you the importance of this situation, Colonel."

"Sir, we'll be on our way tomorrow night, sir."

"No, Colonel. You'll be on your way in the morning. Thank you, gentlemen. Good night."

After they retreated from the admiral's office, Colonel Easy addressed the captain again. "Captain!"

The captain was tiring of the near insubordination of Colonel Easy. "What is it now, Easy?"

Colonel Easy could see the captain was beginning to show a certain amount of disdain for him, and he decided to step a little lighter—but not much. "You know, sir, I'm still not satisfied with the answers. The hair is standing straight up on my neck, and that's a warning I always listen to. I hope I've been given the whole picture—I don't want any surprises."

The captain was nearly ready to bust, not liking the admiral or himself being questioned or second -guessed by a Marine colonel, let alone a smartass corporal. "You heard it from the admiral himself, Colonel. You can't get any higher than he is in this part of the world. He's the man. You might remember who is in charge here, Colonel."

"Yes sir, I'll keep that in mind, but for now, there is something tugging at my shirt sleeve—I'm sure you know the feeling. It says something is missing in the equation. Paying attention to that tingling sensation has saved my ass on numerous occasions and probably will in the future."

While Easy was pumping the captain, the captain received a call and had to leave. Colonel Easy told him he could find his own way back to the flight deck, and as he was about to challenge the stairwells down to the deck, the corporal who was on duty when they arrived at the admiral's quarters requested permission to speak. "Sir, may I have a few words with the Colonel?"

The corporal was showing signs he may have stepped out of bounds, but continued. "I would like the Colonel's advice."

"Speak up, Corporal, what's on your mind?"

"Sir, I have noticed some very unusual behavior by the admiral, and I don't quite know what to do about it. I haven't discussed this with my CO for fear he would call my observations spying, but I think the Colonel would be looking from the outside-in, and have a better perspective."

"All right, Corporal, get on with it—I have a full plate tonight."

"Yes sir, well, it goes like this, sir. Last week when I came into the admiral's quarters, he was reading a letter, which looked like it came from home because the pages were taken from a civilian envelope lying on his desk.

"He didn't hear me when I spoke, so I thought he was caught up in the letter. I spoke a little louder. The admiral still didn't respond or acknowledge my presence. I wanted to get his attention, I walked up to his desk and stood right in front of him. His hands were shaking, and the letter he was reading fell to the deck. Before he picked it up, I could see stamped across the letterhead, in big, bold, red letters, *KENO*. I couldn't see the rest of the pages.

"After a short time, he looked up, startled to see me. He glanced at the letter and slid it into the top middle drawer of his desk. He then said, "What can I do for you, Corporal?"

"I told him the flight officer was waiting outside to accompany the admiral to officer's mess. He replied, "Thank you, Corporal, you may head to chow yourself." He acted like nothing out of the ordinary had taken place. I did an about-face and marched out of his office. The admiral changed just like that, from distant to the here and now, like snapping your fingers."

Colonel Easy was not impressed with the corporal so far. "So big deal, Corporal, he probably got a Dear John and was into its undesirable contents big time."

"But that's not all, sir. Three days ago, I heard him on the phone as I was picking up some orders for the ship's captain. I heard him repeat the word *KENO* twice into the receiver. Then he got all strange again for about five minutes."

"Corporal, tell me again why you're telling me these things about the most powerful man in this part of our world. It sounds like you should be informing your CO, or the chaplain, regardless of what they might think of your motives. I'm sure the chaplain would listen if you think the admiral needs help."

The corporal was becoming as frustrated as the colonel. "Like I said, sir! My CO would think I'm bonkers. Sir, I heard you tell the captain from special operations that the hair was sticking up on your neck, and you usually listen to your instincts. In my combat tour with First Recon, I know what that hair on the neck feels like—I have it also, here and now. There is something fishy about those two F-4s.

"The admiral had two F-4 drivers up here in his quarters; one was Navy and the other a Marine. An ordnance officer came along with them. I wasn't privy to what went on, but when they came out, all three were white as hospital sheets. The ordnance officer was saying, "I don't believe it. I don't believe it." I was relieved about that time, and the next thing I heard was the two F-4s were missing and presumed down. All the events seemed disconnected, but I think there's something very strange going on! The admiral is not himself on occasion. He just goes away somewhere and returns without missing any time. That's it, Colonel."

"Okay, Corporal, I'll look into the matter. In the meantime, keep what we've discussed under wraps. I want you here to keep an eye on the admiral and any unusual happenings. If you go to someone else with it, you'll be relieved."

"Yes sir. How can I contact you, sir?"

"If you think something is very wrong and red-flag serious, contact a Corporal Knight at Third Division HQ. He'll know how to reach me."

"Yes sir."

While Colonel Easy was winding his way down the endless stairwells to the deck, he wondered how the hell he'd got himself into such a convoluted mess. His next move was to contact the ordnance officer just in case the corporal may have stumbled onto something that he would need to know about before shoving off on the operation. If there was something there, it would account for the hair on his neck standing at attention, the tingling sensation bugging him from head to toe.

Colonel Easy found the ordnance officer in the officer's mess, and he was not a happy camper. When he asked him to have a little private conversation about the missing jets, he clammed up like a bank vault at three o'clock, but he did manage to say a few words before he became tongue-tied and lost his hearing. He said everything about the F-4s was top secret and that I should keep those things to myself; I should do whatever the admiral wanted and leave it at that. He then turned away and marched out of the mess.

The demonstration by the ordnance officer made the hair stand up even stiffer. Shit, what the hell was going on here? Well, whatever it was, very few were privy to it, and they weren't talking. With no one left to chat with, he found his way down to the flight deck, hoping the weather had become calm for the ride back to the beach. His next move was to get his troops together and he would deal with what came his way on a first-come, first-serve basis. The carrier was due to leave Yankee Station in a couple of days, and chances were he wouldn't ever see the admiral or captain again. He wasn't impressed about shipboard life; everything was too damned confining. He was also wondering why a sub-hunter carrier was sitting off shore anyway. Last he heard the NVA didn't have any subs, and the Russians were not that close to shore.

USMC

CHAPTER 4

Scout Sniper Platoon Area

After fifteen tries, Primrose finally got through to Rhonda. Using the phone system in the Far East was like playing Russian roulette: you never knew when you'd hit the jackpot and blow your brains out. Usually you got whoever the operator decided to hook you up with. It could be a bus station in Bangkok or a whorehouse in Calcutta. Lucky for him, he got the number he wanted.

"Rhonda."

"Yes, hello Zach, nice to hear your voice, are you getting away for a while?"

"No, but it sure would be nice to hold you and look into those beautiful eyes. I had a new mission presented to me. If I accept, I can extend my tour. That would fit into our plans, so I'm going to take it. The mission will require that I get in touch with O, McPotts, and Ourdae, like, yesterday! "

"No sweat, Zach, they're downstairs in the bar as we speak. But by now they will be about two sheets to the wind. You might want to wait until they sober up—if you know what I mean."

"We can't wait, Rhonda. Get them upstairs with some hot coffee or whatever it takes to straighten them up. I need them bright-eyed and bushy-tailed as fast as you can."

"Okay, honey, but you know how they are!"

Primrose could see Rhonda trying to get the three reprobates under control. They would listen to her way before they would listen to their old sergeant.

"I know, tell them it's life or death for a whole bunch of Marines if they don't get their shit together."

"Okay, I'll go downstairs and round them up."

"Rhonda, please call me as soon as they can make sense of anything. I love you."

"I'll call when they can stand up without assistance. I love you too. Ciao."

Damn, he needed those guys sober right away. Why does Murphy always stick his ugly head up when you least expect it or need it? He'd better get the rest of the motley crew together or at least put them on short notice for a mission. Toms would already be out for the night, collecting his gruesome ears and fmgers. Martin and Knight were here, no problem. Champion was in the brig, and the newly pinned Lieutenant may be able to spring him without the colonel's help. Slipps was over at the combat engineers compound, trading something he got from the Seabees. He'd said something about trading penicillin, because the Seabees had the highest VD rate in I-Corps. He could pick him up in the morning.

Primrose wondered if the colonel wanted Heto, the tracker? He'd better give him a heads-up just in case. Heto was the best jungle tracker in the world, and he hoped the colonel wanted him on the team again. The colonel wouldn't stiff him like the CIA had in the past. Primrose wondered why Division wanted their motley crew for this particular operation. The higher-ups had plenty of super-snoopers—or, more to the point— pooper snoopers—if they didn't like the odds. The operation must be too dangerous for them—just like the last time they called on the colonel—they would send it the dumbass Marine grunts to do their dirty work.

In any case, the first thing on his agenda would be to relieve the brig of Champion, for he'd be more difficult to get back into the fold. He wondered what the hell he'd done this time. He couldn't turn his back on those jarheads for one lousy minute without them getting into the shit again! Maybe if he hustled over to the brig, he might get Champion released right away. If not, the colonel would have to take care of that problem.

As he walked up to the brig, it reminded him of an old backlot of a western movie set, with the bad guys in black hats pulling the bars from the rear windows with their horses. The team may have to spring Champion, if they don't get any cooperation from the turnkey. The brig looked pretty porous; it would probably be an easy hit.

As he neared the brig, he could see the big turnkey; he didn't look happy about his job or life in general.

He introduced himself. "Sergeant, my name is lieutenant Primrose. I've come to see one of my Marines you've got locked up here; his name is Champion."

The sergeant looked like a club fighter who could handle himself in any situation. He retorted, "Yes sir, he's here and a real pain in the ass. The guy you seem to be so proud of has made threats to blow up my brig with everyone in it. As you can see, that wouldn't take much—I told him anyone who could walk and talk would be able to drop this place, no problem. He replied that he would be doing us a favor to implode the brig, even though it was beneath his talent level to destroy such a poorly constructed building. He added that if he imploded the brig, everyone could see it go up in smoke. If he left it alone, it would collapse all by itself, and no one would know when that was going to happen."

Primrose gave the turnkey all the time he needed to vent about Champion before he asked, "All that aside, Sergeant, what's he in for?"

"Sir, you need to speak with the OD, Captain Weakly. Champion's rap sheet is extensive, and he may be in for some big-time shit. The death of two French Special Forces guys is involved. I'll get the captain for you. Please have a seat, Lieutenant I'll be right back."

When the officer of the day came through the door with the sergeant, Primrose observed that his name was perfect. He looked like the class nerd, with the homed-rimmed glasses and that ambulance-chaser lawyer attitude. He had a squeaky voice to match his appearance. He said, "Lieutenant Primrose, I'm Captain Weakly. How may I help you?"

Primrose would have rather dealt with the brig sergeant than the nerd standing before him. "Sir, you have one of my men confined here, and I've come to see about having him released."

"According to the sergeant, you're referring to a grunt name of Champion?"

"Yes sir, my CO needs him for a special mission. He has some unusual talent that is needed immediately. Would you mind giving me an overview of the charges against him?"

"Lieutenant, you don't seem to understand the situation here. The charges are too many for a quick overview, but you are welcome to read them from the legal-sized folders. They list all his offenses—help yourself."

Primrose was getting pissed at the captain dragging his feet, so with a more forceful tone he said, "Captain, how about you just give me a brief synopsis of his charges, so I can relay them to the battalion commander Lieutenant Colonel Easy. I'm sure he would appreciate your candor. What has he done to piss off so many people?"

"Okay, Lieutenant, it goes like this: To start with, there were two Brits, two Aussies, one Marine and two French Special Forces people at the Enlisted Men's Club. At present there are two Brits, two Aussies, and one Marine who we have locked up here."

Primrose wished the turnkey could have filled him in on the situation. The captain was using his lawyer talk, and it was going to take forever to get the skinny on Champion.

"From the reports, the festivities began at the EM Club. After a fair amount of adult beverages had been consumed, one thing led to another, with the Aussies saying the Marines are all show and no go. The Brits backed up the Aussies and the French naturally remained neutral. Champion, not one to back off, challenged the lot of them to see whose ass is hiding in the trenches and whose isn't. He says he knows of a firebase not far away that gets pounded every night at 2300 with mortar fire that is heavy and on time.

"Champion suggests they all go over there and when the incoming starts, they all run out and dodge the fireworks: running from one end of the base to the other, and whoever doesn't make it, tough shit. He says that will separate the all show and no go from the real men—the Marines!

"There is a show of hands, and the blurry-eyed group of dipshits agree to the test. So they head out, looking for transportation, and the dumbasses run across an unattended six-by. The French S/F guys jump in the cab and drive while Champion gives directions from the back with the others. The French troopers don't understand much English, but follow the arm waving of your guy. They had two minor accidents on the way, and they are hit and run cases.

"When the shit-faced group arrives at the firebase, Champion tells the guards that he has six international forces there to observe how the defenses are set up for regular nightly mortar fire at the base. The guard, knowing the mortar fire is about to start dropping in, doesn't argue. He waves the truck in and warns them of the impending barrage. He suggests they take cover just below the flagpole as he's heading at full stride for the nearest bunker.

"Frenchy drives the truck to the suggested parking place and everyone dismounts and gets ready to run from end to end when the thump, thump starts. The first round comes damn close to the group, and the French guys dive under the truck while the rest of them start running across the base. They're all laughing like they've gone fucking nuts! Well, guess what? The gooks train their mortars on the six-by, figuring it's bringing in replacements and ammunition. They walk their mortars right up to the truck. Because the mortar fire was right on target, the Frogs are now missing two Special Forces troopers. The others come running back to help, but the six-by is just a pile of twisted metal; it doesn't even look like a truck. The two Frogs could have been gathered up and put in a sock.

"The base commander, after finding out what the hell happened, was on the verge of having the lot of them lined up and shot. The battalion sergeant major stepped in and saved their sorry asses from execution. The CO had them all chained together and hauled down to the brig here with instructions to have them hanged by the neck until dead—at sunrise. I believe if the CO has his way, Champion will die without a blindfold.

"The Aussies and the Brits were from a group training offshore, and they were released to their respective CO's, who were to bring them back to face charges once the legal whirlpool found its way through the muck and mire of an international incident. In reality, those troops were put on a plane, and I'm sure they are drinking beer down under and in merry old England, never to be seen again.

"The powers that be want your guy for stealing government property, destroying same, traveling without authorization, using false verbal orders, breaching a secure area, endangering military personnel and equipment, and creating an international incident, along with being AWOL! There are other charges, but that pretty much covers it for now. There are two bright spots in Champion's favor. Number one, the French guy was driving the truck, so he basically stole it, and he's dead, along with his partner. Number two, the Brits and Aussies are long gone, so there are no witnesses to testify against him. Chances are he may skate the whole fucking event, because the brass may want to sweep the affair under the rug. The only problem is telling the French how two of their finest were blown up at a firebase they weren't supposed to be at, and that's a Division problem. I'll know what to do with Champion in the morning. So there you have it, Lieutenant."

"Sir, my CO will be in touch in the morning."

"One other thing, Lieutenant: the CO of the firebase has now gotten the motor pool to give him all their unrepairable trucks and other vehicles. He puts them around the firebase in harmless places, and the gooks shell the shit out of them every night and leave the rest of the place alone.

"He said to thank Champion for the idea, but if he ever sees him again, he'll strap him to the perimeter wire so the enemy sappers can blow his ass up."

Primrose couldn't believe the bunch of fuckups on Easy's payroll. Would their quest never end to see who could be the worst pain in the ass on the planet? It would be good to get back in the bush and do what the team did best. The colonel would not be happy about Champion, but then he wasn't happy about much of anything unless he was in the jungle leading Marines in combat.

At daylight, when Primrose finally got everybody together and lined up on the road in front of the colonel's tent, he announced, "Sir, all present or accounted for."

"Thank you, Lieutenant," the colonel said, as he stood in front of the makeshift battalion office. "I'm going to check on Champion." He did an about-face and headed in the direction of the brig.

The accounted-for also included Toms, who wasn't present, but whose whereabouts was common knowledge. Toms was out killing the enemy and gathering trophies on his own terms. He would return at sunrise to get indoors and avoid the daylight in order to preserve his night vision.

Primrose dismissed the formation with orders to be on the road in one hour to mount the trucks and get a briefing from the colonel. If Champion took longer to get released, the colonel would do the briefing on the tarmac, before they boarded for the ride south.

Primrose had one hour to get in touch with Rhonda for an update on the brown-water sailors. She hadn't called back, so he figured they were still too wasted to make any sense. After fifteen minutes of the allotted hour, he heard the sweet sound of her voice, "Hello, this is Rhonda." He tingled at the sound of her voice. "Hi Rhonda. Did you get those guys to answer up?"

"Zach, yes, and I gave them a brief outline as you told me. They agreed it was a good opportunity for them to get squared away with the world."

"Are they there right now?"

"Yes."

"Please put McPotts on."

"McPotts, did you understand what Rhonda was explaining to you three clowns?"

"Why are you being so calm and understanding, Lieutenant?"

"Look, McPotts, this is one hell of a good offer! Do you guys want in or not? We don't have time to be fucking around. Yes or no?"

"Yes sir, we want in. I speak for O and Ourdae—we're ready to sign on."

"Good. Now listen: have the boat ready; we'll be there ASAP. The mission may be back into the same area as the last time. Top off the tanks and put all the firepower you can on board. This will probably be a dicey, tight-ass operation."

"Yes sir. Semper Fi. We'll be squared away and standing tall on the dock, ready for action when you arrive."

Primrose didn't buy any of that shit for a minute. It wasn't in those birds to be squared away.

CHAPTER 5

Scout Sniper Platoon Area: Mount Out

Primrose stood in the middle of the area counting heads and found all present but Toms, whom he could see dragging his ass in from the bush. Figuring out Toms was difficult at best. One wondered how he managed to always win. Anyone would be happy to be half as good. The bounty on him and Martin had doubled in the past six months.

Primrose pulled Toms aside and asked, "How was the hunt, my Indian friend?

"I made the Corps proud of me, Lieutenant, with three kills last night. Wanna see the results?"

"Not particularly, but the colonel might. He has a special mission on tap, and he wants the same crew as last time to join him. Would you be interested?"

"Hell yeah, I'm interested, but I was out all night and need a good day's sleep."

"Sorry pal; if you want in, you can sleep on the chopper."

"Crap, not another chopper ride! As you know, Lieutenant, I don't soar like eagle, no matter what the shamans say about brave Indian warriors. It's pretty important, huh?"

"Toms, there is nothing more important on anybody's agenda than this operation."

They were all standing tall on the road in front of the colonel's tent when he returned with Champion in tow. Champion was not smiling, and the colonel was straight-faced. Primrose wondered what the colonel had to give up to spring Champion. The colonel said, "Listen up! Everyone gather in the tent."

They all stumbled into the close quarters of the tent.

The colonel was enthusiastic as he addressed his team of misfits. "Gentlemen, everything heard in this meeting is considered top secret and to be treated accordingly. Nothing I share with you will be repeated by word of mouth or any other form of communication.

"We've been selected for a job that'll require our combined combat skills. Division's choosing of our team was based on our proven track record and willingness to complete the mission, no matter the conditions. The mission is to locate the remains of two F-4 Phantoms; they are down somewhere in this area."

The colonel was pointing his swagger stick at a map of Cambodia. He continued, "This is the general area where Division and the Navy think they disappeared. As you can see, it's near the area where we were, last time out. McPotts, O and Ourdae are standing by with the PT, and McPotts will be able to put us right on target. There will be two C-47 Sky-trains on the tarmac warmed up and waiting. They will fly us over to Phnom Penh, where we'll meet the PT and the brown-water guys at the old hangar on the river, from our last mission. From there we'll motor up the Mekong, locate the jets, retrieve what's worth keeping, along with the pilots, and then Champion will blow what's left into confetti. Oh—and one more thing: if the pilots are not dead, but captured, we will rescue them. I'll go into what each of you will be responsible for when we get airborne or at the hangar on the river. Now fall out and get your gear ready to mount up—the trucks are on the way."

When the trucks arrived, they loaded their gear and bodies in record time.

The colonel was standing there yelling like a boot camp drill instructor at their every move. He had that gleam in his eyes that told the team he was ready to lead them into combat.

The colonel was a pure warrior, a man in the right place at the right time.

They boarded the old C-47 relics, which were DC-Dakotas, converted for troop transport. They were happy to be in an aircraft, that when modified further, became an AC-47 gunship, nicknamed "Spooky" or "Puff the Magic Dragon," an aircraft that made the enemy quiver and duck for cover when they saw one coming in low with its mini-guns blazing away.

The plane soared off the runway in the direction of Cambodia with the colonel yelling above the noise of the engines about their mission in more detail. Toms was happy the chopper ride had turned into a plane ride: he was lots better with wings than blades. Martin was cleaning his rifle with the care one would give a fine watch or diamond. That sniper rifle had been cleaned so many times it operated with the precision of a fine Swiss clock. Its performance had never failed him in combat. Sniping is a high-risk operation, with failure not an option. Champion looked like he was praying, and Primrose wondered what the colonel had done to make him bow his head in prayer. Slipps was listening intently to the colonel, along with the rest of the team. The colonel kept repeating that there were many new super high-tech weapons on the downed jets.

As Primrose was trying to hear over the noise of the engines, he remembered he had forgotten to ask about getting Heto the tracker on the team. They might need the talent of a genius like him in the jungle they'd be encountering. Between Heto and Toms, they had the best trackers in all of the Far East.

Getting Heto wouldn't be a problem. Rhonda could contact him on a landline from Phnom Penh, and he wouldn't have any trouble getting a hop from Okinawa. He had the Air Force by the ass for one reason or another, which he wouldn't share.

Knight was grinning from ear to ear. He was finally going on an operation from the get go. After he had threatened to spill the beans on their checkered past, the colonel agreed to bring him along. Primrose hoped nothing bad happened to him; good guys like Knight were hard to find.

CHAPTER 6

Phnom Penh, Cambodia

The trucks were waiting for them on the tarmac in Phnom Penh. After deplaning, they loaded their gear on the old six-bys and headed for the dock area. Toms nodded out again, and they all marveled at his talent to sleep whenever and wherever he chose!

Colonel Easy remarked, "It will be good to see the rogue pirates again, even though the three are a commander's nightmare. The best thing about those three is their expertise in combat. You don't have to look around and wonder if they are there. One other thing for sure—there is never a dull moment!" The team all nodded in agreement.

Colonel Easy and Primrose discussed how and from where they'd run their base of operations. Because of the good location of the Dragonfly Bar and Hotel where Rhonda was staying, it was decided to establish the command post at the hotel. There was an abundance of landlines and a high antenna at the top of the penthouse. With all the traffic in and out of the hotel and bar, they wouldn't be conspicuous. The embassy, on the other hand, was constantly monitored by the enemy and even their own brass, who would be rubbernecking their every move.

When they arrived at the old dock hangar, there were lots of smiles and handshakes. The three rogues were really happy to see old faces, and visa versa. The colonel remarked, "Nice to see your ugly mugs again. We've not heard much of you lately, and what we did hear was all bad."

O retorted, "Well sir, we've had to keep a low profile due to a rather involved situation that Ourdea and McPotts got us into. Their asses are in a sling over some woman they found up river."

Colonel Easy wanted to impress upon O and the other two how serious the situation was. With his forehead wrinkled up nicely he said, "Look, O, I don't care one shit about you and your two butthead friends' female adventures. What we need now is total commitment for the mission ahead. Do you read me?"

O responded, "Yes sir, loud and clear."

Easy softened a little as he noticed the PT. "I see the PT is loaded for bear! I'm impressed with your effort to get the boat ready and being stone-ass sober. Outstanding job gentlemen."

The PT was purring like a contented cat after downing a can of tuna. The crew did have a serious side to their personalities after all. Cleaning up the boat and themselves indicated that they wanted to take the colonel's offer to amend for their past fuckups!

"Gather around, gentlemen, and listen up! I'm going over this again for the benefit of those not present the first go-around. Primrose, hang the map there on the bulkhead."

"Yes sir."

The colonel singled out O, Ourdae, and McPotts. "This is for your benefit. The rest of the team was briefed before we shoved off."

He had a slight grin on his otherwise straight face, as he pointed his swagger stick at a map of Cambodia. Colonel Easy was in his element now, and it was obvious the adrenalin was in high gear.

"McPotts, do you see any problems getting the team into this area?"

"No sir, but it's thick-ass jungle shit!"

"Thank you, McPotts. According to the satellite photos, there is no evidence of a crash site like there should be. Those two should have left a football-field sized splash in the jungle, but nothing has been discovered."

Ourdae, spoke up. "Sir."

"Speak, Ourdae," the colonel said, in the manner of a drill instructor.

"Sir, what makes the brass think they went down inland that far?"

"Ourdae, they disappeared from radar in this area on the map. With their airspeed and altitude, X marks the spot most likely to be the crash site."

"Sir?"

"Yes, Toms."

Toms looked directly into the colonel's eyes. "Sir, they didn't crash."

The colonel was incredulous, "What do you mean, they didn't crash?"

"I had a dream, but I didn't put it together until now. The shamans sent me stuff in a dream that the F-4s landed and didn't plow into the jungle."

"Toms, there are no landing strips anywhere near this area. I hate to bust your bubble, but the shamans are wrong!"

"Sir, the shamans are never wrong, only stiff-necked white men are wrong!"

The colonel was becoming testy with Toms. "Toms, aerial photos have been taken, along with the satellite stuff, and there are no tarmacs anywhere near this area. What the hell do you need to understand? The F-4s didn't land in this jungle terrain. Jesus!"

Toms wasn't about to give up on his shamans. "Believe me, Colonel, they didn't crash. They landed!"

"Shit, Toms, listen: there are no landing strips in the area, period."

"Sir, then they landed somewhere else, not in that area. We'll be looking in the wrong place." The colonel turned away from Toms and continued, pointing to the map. "As I was saying, gentlemen, we'll boat up to Kompong Chan, which will put us in this area."

Moving the swagger stick, he added, "From there we'll push into the jungle and locate the crash site."

Toms made one last effort to get the attention of the colonel, "No crash site, sir."

"Toms, leave it alone! Drop it!"

"Yes sir."

Colonel Easy continued, "Now men, this is how it'll be. We'll locate the crash site, recover the bodies and all retrievable electronic gear, and anything else of value that we can carry out. Champion and Slipps will destroy what is left. Then we'll load up and head back downriver. Once we're back in Phnom Penh, we'll catch our C-47s and fly back to Da Nang for our rewards on a job well done.

"Just a note: the electronics gear is supposedly state of the art and could have accounted for the downing of the jets. The stuff may have had some glitch in it, and down they went!

"All our radio contact will be in code. My call sign will be Popeye, and yours Sailor. We'll set up our command post in the Dragonfly Bar and Hotel. Rhonda is playing there as you know, and it'll be good cover, along with a nice high aerial on the top of the penthouse. I'll be at the Dragonfly to keep communications flowing, and I want contact—lots of contact. Use a land line when possible.

"You know about where to start, Primrose, so mount up and shove off."

"Yes sir."

"I want a radio message as soon as you locate the site. Just radio *Bonanza;* that's what I'll be waiting to hear."

"Yes sir."

As soon as they boarded the PT, Colonel Easy headed for the Dragonfly. With Rhonda's help, the bar would become a very busy CP and communications center.

The colonel wanted Knight to stay back and help with communications, but he threw such a fit he let him go with the team. Knight was going to go, come hell or high water!

As they shoved off, Toms could be heard muttering that the two jets didn't crash. Because of past exploits, the colonel usually took what Toms said to heart. The crew was surprised he hadn't listened this time and had cut Toms off so abruptly.

O took the PT out to the middle of the Mekong, and they cruised upstream towards the Kompong Cham. The team, now a crew, were glad to be back on the brown water, for it had some good memories, with a few battles won and many narrow escapes. Due to the reputation of the PT and its motley crew, they had to man their weapons continually.

How the PT crew slept at night would make an interesting study for a team of shrinks, because it wasn't only the river pirates looking to capture the PT, there was the matter of a warlord's daughter who was thought to have been compromised by one the three rogues. Along with all that there was the real enemy—the VC and NVA—to consider. And the enemy was still pissed off because the PT had captured their suitcase nuclear bombs and kicked their slimy little asses up and down the Mekong. The PT had someone on its trail all the time, which kept everyone alert, bright-eyed and bushy-tailed.

"Rhonda."

"Yes, Colonel."

"We need to get in touch with the American Embassy here. Toms was saying something about dreams from the shamans that didn't make any sense. He's usually right about this stuff. Do you have a friend in the embassy?"

"Yes, the secretary to the ambassador."

"Is she a good friend? Someone you can pick up the phone and call?"

"Yes, we are very good fiends. I'll call the embassy."

While they waited for the embassy call to go through, Colonel Easy continued. "Toms has me rethinking this whole mission concept. The Marine who was an admiral's orderly on the carrier *Hornet,* where I received the briefing on the operation told me some strange and disturbing things about the admiral's behavior. The hair on my neck is calling me again. That's a sign to take another look at things past, present, and future. The whole series of events just doesn't add up. Nothing fits. Someone is holding out on us! Maybe your friend can help us."

"Colonel, the embassy is on the line." said Rhonda, as she returned her attention to the phone.

"Hello Cleo, this is Rhonda. How are things?"

"We're fine here, and how's the entertainment business?"

"Working steady, between Phnom Penh, Bangkok, and Hong Kong. Not bad for a girl from the States. I have a request, if you would be so kind."

"Sure, Rhonda, shoot."

"Cleo, I have a Lieutenant. Colonel Easy here. He would like to ask you about the Kompong Cham area."

"Sure, Rhonda. I'm familiar with the area. Put the colonel on."

"Hello, Cleo, this is Colonel Easy. Thanks for taking my call, it's important for my mission here."

Cleo liked the sound of Easy's voice and felt comfortable with him. "I'm glad to help, Colonel; I grew up around Kompong Cham."

"Cleo, were you in the area during the war when the Japanese were in control?"

"Yes, but I was very young. My whole family lived there during the occupation."

"Do you remember if the Japanese had any large facilities in the area, maybe an airfield?"

"Colonel, I remember lots of Japanese Zeros in the sky, but never thought much about where they came from or disappeared to. I don't know about airfields, but I'll check the archives here. If I don't find anything, I'll get in touch with my father and uncle—they would know. I may have something by tomorrow."

"Thanks, Cleo. Whatever you can do will be a great help to us, thank you."

"Colonel, may I ask why you are looking for an old Japanese airstrip?"

"No, Cleo, but when this mission is finished, I'll fill you in on the details. Working at the embassy, I'm sure your security clearance is high, but this is even over my head."

"I do have a high clearance, Colonel. Would you put Rhonda back on, please?"

"Thanks, Cleo, here's Rhonda."

The colonel handed the phone to Rhonda and shrugged his shoulders—like maybe she had helped.

"Rhonda, we should have lunch this week, so you can give me your engagement schedule for the month. I want to take a week and spend some time at the beach in Bangkok. I'd like to go when you're playing."

"Ten-four Cleo! Bye—and thanks."

As the PT was heading upriver, the team, now part of the crew, were going over all the possibilities that may come their way.

Primrose asked Slipps, "Do you know anything about the latest night vision equipment on a jet aircraft?"

"No sir, I haven't heard or seen anything new since I've been in-country" Slipps answered, wondering about the question, more apt to be addressed to a wing wiper.

"How about something that absorbs radar and doesn't send images back?"

"No sir, nothing about that either."

Primrose continued with the questions, hoping to get a maybe. "How about something that makes radar bounce off and give false readings?"

"Nope. Sir, I'm a weapons expert, remember! I don't know much about the sophisticated aircraft of today."

"Yes I know, Slipps. I was just thinking out loud."

"Lieutenant Primrose!"

"Yes, Toms, what is it this time?"

Toms was getting a little irritated with all the negativity towards him, but pushed on with his assertions. "Sir, I'm deadass serious about those jets not slamming into the jungle floor. The shamans are never wrong, as I said to the colonel, and my interpretation of the dream is correct. There is something fishy about this mission. My whole body is tingling for attention. I can feel it and smell it, and it's rotten. we're blind to it. I'm passing on the warning I received.

"We haven't been told the whole story, and there are surprises coming our way. The team needs to be vigilant because our back door is open.

"Other than that, sir, this could be a great adventure, although I was a little confused with the colonel's attitude about my dreams. Our past history should have been enough for him to take the warnings seriously."

"I agree, Toms. Keep me posted if you receive anymore information, and we'll take extra care on our six."

CHAPTER 7

The WarLords

The PT and its crew were well on their way up the river when O yelled out to Primrose, "Lieutenant, we have a problem."

Primrose knew the river was too quiet, given the PT's reputation. "What's the problem, O?"

"Up ahead there are a bunch of boats strung across the river. Do you see them?"

"Yeah, so what? There's a million boats on the Mekong."

"Sir, those particular boats are flying the colors of a warlord who isn't fond of McPotts, Ourdae, or me. They may want to get even for a few things that happened over the past few months. We don't usually come this far upriver. It's kind of a mutual agreement. They stay up north, and we stay down south. The PT and its crew are now in violation of that agreement. The lieutenant can try to negotiate our way upriver or maybe buy safe passage without confrontation. Then again, we could just blast our way through. But either way, the pirates will want some kind of payment. The payment could be in blood or money—they're not picky, but it's usually blood. They're really pissed at us right now!"

Primrose was not surprised by anything O had said, "O, you conveniently forgot to mention this little problem before we headed upriver!"

"Yes sir, its just one of many I haven't gotten around to sharing. It kinda slipped my mind."

"O, lots of things seem to have slipped your mind."

O wanted to get past the present dialogue and asked, "What will it be, Lieutenant, talk or fight?"

"Let's try to negotiate a deal for a few bucks and be on our way."

"Okay sir, but they're shrewd traders. You need to be on your toes."

"I'm not going to talk to them, Toms is. What do you think, Toms? Can you use your Indian trading skills to get us upriver?"

"Yes sir, no problem, piece of cake for old Indian trader like me."

When the PT was nearly a hundred yards from the boats blocking the river, Toms waved a white flag, jumped into a rubber dinghy, and paddled out to meet the pirate's lead boat. From the PT they could see, but not hear, an animated conversation ensuing, with lots of arm and hand waving. A couple of times it looked like Toms was about to shoot their leader, and visa versa. After much rocking of both boats, Toms shook hands with their leader, and the pirates came about with their boats. The river was once again open to

56

through traffic heading north. There were smiles all around as the pirates spread out to give them room. O kept the PT a safe distance, not trusting the river pirates.

Toms paddled the dinghy to the stern of the PT, where he was pulled aboard from the little boat. He was smiling and very proud of himself as he said, "That was simple enough, Lieutenant, all the pirates wanted were the three assholes here on the boat who've been giving them fits all up and down the river. They don't want our boat, weapons, or anything else, just O, McPotts, and Ourdae. The leader told me they want to tie theirs arms between two boats and pull them apart. The leader's translator was having a hard time with my words, but we did reach an understanding.

"I told him the three rogues were under arrest, and we're taking them upriver to recover some stolen property. The leader said the property probably belonged to him, and he wanted it back. Being very firm, I told him we'd hand the three over to them on the way back downriver. I suggested it would save the U. S. Government a shitload of money not putting them on trial. I confirmed that our leader thought they should punish them rather than us. The pirates liked the sound of that, and to cement the deal, I gave the permission to blow us out of the water if my words weren't true. They had seen Western movies and knew Indians never lie.

"I think they would love to get the three rogues off the boat, kill them, and then blow us to smithereens, somewhere on our journey downriver."

Primrose looked at Toms and said, "Nice going, Toms. You gave them permission to sink us!"

"Sir, you asked me to negotiate our passage upriver, nothing was said about coming back downriver."

"Okay, Toms, good job, we can worry about that little problem on the return trip. McPotts what did you guys do to piss these fellows off?"

"Sir, it's a long story."

"That's fine, McPotts, I want to hear it." said Lieutenant Primrose as he settled back in the captain's chair to hear the cock-and-bull story that was coming.

"Sir, have you heard of the ambition to rob someone who had just robbed someone?"

"Can't say that I have, McPotts. Sounds like an oxymoron."

"Well, we stumbled upon our friends out there hijacking a boat loaded with precious gems. They had just relieved a commercial trading boat of their cargo, so when they made their getaway, we intercepted them and lifted the booty. It was a one-sided affair because we're better pirates than they are. Bottom line is, they couldn't say shit about being robbed of their ill-gotten goods. We sold half the gems, and stashed the other half for the future.

"Those sorry fuckers were a little put out about the whole matter. We can't figure why they're so angry. Had the situation been reversed, they'd have done the same thing to us. Business is business. What really is the cause of the irritation may be the fact that we sent four of their prime boats to the bottom of the river in the process of taking possession of the cargo. That may have been a little much, kinda over the top."

Primrose shook his head in amazement that the three were still breathing. "McPotts, I get the feeling these people may not be the only ones on the river we have to look out for! Do you agree?"

"Yes sir, I think you may consider the river a hostile environment where we are concerned."

"Do you rogues have any friends on the river, or only enemies?"

"Sir, we have many friends. They just don't show up as often as the bad guys."

"Just off the top of your head, McPotts, can you think of anyone we have to worry about for the rest of the trip north?"

"Not right offhand, sir."

"Lieutenant Primrose."

"Yes, O."

"Sir, when we get to Kompong Cham, there is a little bar on the waterfront where we can tie up on the dock right in front of the place. There may be lots of information floating around from the river people, due to the abundance of boat traffic there and in the area we're going to search. I can't imagine those F-4s going down with no one hearing or seeing them. If the river people found the crash site, there will be nothing left for us to find. The boat people would've picked the crash site clean. There should be some word going around if two American jets went plowing into the jungle anywhere nearby."

CHAPTER 8

The Dragonfly Bar and Hotel

Rhonda was manning the radio and phones while the colonel was out, and sure enough it got busy.

"Hello, this is Rhonda."

"Rhonda, this is Cleo. I have some information for the colonel in reference to our conversation the other day."

"He's not in right now, Cleo, but he should be back in an hour or so. Is it something I can relay to the colonel?"

"No, Rhonda. I'll come by the Dragonfly in the morning. Some of the things I have to tell him should be eye to eye."

"Okay. Thanks, Cleo. I'll tell the colonel when he returns."

Damn! Every time the colonel leaves the building, the phone and radio come to life. Rhonda was getting the full measure of what it took to be the center of communications. Murphy was always in the wings waiting to dump on someone. But she'd had a call from O, who wanted to test the two-way, just in case it was the only way to keep in touch. And it had been nice to hear Zach's voice when he called to let the colonel know they'd arrived in Kompong Cham. He had mentioned that Rhonda should make plans to hit the beach when the mission was over and then spend a weekend in Hong Kong. Rhonda had agreed. Her group had been working six months straight.

The colonel didn't return until the following morning. He knocked three times rapidly and then twice slowly for the code to enter the penthouse. When Rhonda opened the door, she saw a weird look on his face. "Good morning, Colonel." He smiled and said the trip had been worthwhile.

Rhonda told him that Cleo had called and wanted to meet for breakfast. The Colonel replied, "I can imagine what she's going to tell me. I talked to the old men down by the docks, and they seem to remember a seldom-used airstrip in the area we are concerned about. They thought the jungle overgrowth would have made it unusable over the years. The old guys said there are still Japanese soldiers running around creating havoc; they don't believe the war is over. They are still fighting, and sometimes they are deadly. No one seems able to track them down, and because the area is so isolated, the government doesn't think they're worth the trouble to rein in. Just another fly in the ointment. Are you ready to head down to breakfast?"

"Sure, Cleo should be here anytime."

The waiter seated them by a window overlooking the street. They would be able to see Cleo coming down the sidewalk: she wouldn't be hard to pick out of a crowd. Cleo was tall, blonde, and very French, the offspring of a Swedish father and a French-Cambodian mother. The woman was stunning and cunning, with a couple of side businesses in addition to her position at the embassy. Her father and mother stayed in the background and handled her everyday business affairs. Her shrewd business sense had made her family wealthy and respected throughout the Far East.

"There she is now, Colonel."

Easy had seen beautiful women all over the world, but nothing like Cleo. "Damn, if you aren't right on the money. She is stunning! Is she married?"

"No, she can't seem to find anyone who can keep up with her."

"Well, I might like to take up that challenge—she's in a league all her own."

Cleo waved at Rhonda from the entrance, and the waiter led her over to their table.

"Cleo, you look great."

"Thank you, Rhonda."

"Cleo, this is Colonel Easy."

Easy wasn't the type to try and dazzle a beautiful woman with a phony display of bravado. He simply remarked, "It's my pleasure to meet you, Cleo, and thank you for taking the time to help us out."

Colonel Easy noticed how gracious Cleo was with her movements and the flow of her speech. He was impressed more and more as she spoke.

"Colonel, I'm happy to help you in any way that I can. I don't think much of the people you're in conflict with. They are a group of savages who haven't gotten over the Japanese losing the war. The river pirates were ring kissers for the Japs, who used the scumbags as their henchmen to terrorize the locals and keep them in line. When the Japs left, there was no one to pay them for their low-life deeds, so their next move was to join the Communist movement.

"What I have to tell you is both interesting and scary at the same time. There is an old WWII airfield in the area you mentioned. It was used to send planes out to bomb the Burma Road. Because it was used by bombers, it's quite long and could handle most of today's jet aircraft. Whether the field is usable or not, I don't know. My father and uncle were in the area during the war, in a POW camp near the field. My mom, grandmother, and I hid at an old French plantation during the war and managed to keep out of harm's way for the duration. When my father and uncle were taken prisoner, the Japs also confiscated their businesses. When the war ended, they got their shops back, but the scars of the POW camp still remain. The henchmen the Japs used are still around, and there are some Jap soldiers who haven't surrendered. They are still out in the jungle fighting the war."

"Yes, Cleo, I learned about the field and the Japanese soldiers from a couple of old-timers near the docks. It all falls right in with the other stories I've heard. Your confirmation ties it all up for me, and I can't thank you enough."

Cleo nodded and added, "One more thing, Colonel: this brown envelope contains the coordinates of the bomber airstrip."

"Cleo, that is great news. Now we won't have to spend God knows how much time searching for the field. We can move in quickly, no needle in the haystack this time out. Again Cleo, thank you. How about cocktails and dinner, you choose the place. Rhonda will join us, of course."

"That sounds good, Colonel, I accept—and Colonel, I may be of some assistance from the embassy. Please allow me to support you from there when I can."

"Cleo, that means I'll owe you more than one dinner, but for now, how about breakfast?"

"I would be delighted, Colonel, I'm starving."

"I think she likes you, Colonel."

Colonel Easy let a slight smile come across his lips as he remarked, "Well, it would be too much to hope for. I would certainly like to get to know her a lot better. Since her information confirmed what I learned, it's time to contact 'Sailor' and pass on the good news. Did you say they radioed and also called on a landline?"

"Yes, Colonel. They called from a riverfront bar in Kompong Cham."

The colonel's forehead wrinkled as he remembered the weakness the PT crew had for the bar scene. "That figures. Those guys have a fatal disease—bar-itis. They shouldn't be let out without adult supervision. Let's go up to the penthouse and give them a shout."

"Sailor, Sailor, this is Popeye, do you read me? Over. They tried for an hour without a response.

Rhonda, said, "Let's try a landline, Colonel! I'll make the call. No one will be listening in on a woman, and I'll speak their language."

She dialed up the number and didn't have to wait long, before she heard, "Hello, Stateside Bar and Grill."

"Hello, I'm looking for Sailor. Is he around?"

The woman who answered sounded young, and Rhonda wondered if she was the bartender or office help. The young woman said, "One moment, please."

"Colonel, I got through to the bar. It must be owned by an American who is either retired or a deserter. I haven't heard of the place before, and this kind of bar usually gets known quickly, up and down the river. Whoever answered the phone spoke perfect English."

"Leave it to McPotts to open a bar for future retirement opportunities and a second or third source of income."

66

"Hold on, Colonel, Sailor is on the line."

Rhonda was happy to hear Zach's voice. She asked, "Zach, can we talk?"

"Hello to you too."

"Sorry Zach, but business first."

"Sure, we can talk. This is as secure a line as one can get in this part of the world, installed by none other than McPotts."

"Popeye is here to talk. I love you."

"Me too."

"Sailor, are you finished with your love life? Can we get on with the important shit now?"

"Yes sir."

"Listen closely, Sailor. We have a home plate to go for. Home plate was once on a good playing field. Long balls could be hit there, lots of field. When the visiting team left, there were some players who stayed behind. They are still playing. The score for the last game will be coming over the air, and only that score will be broadcast. The score numbers should put you at home plate. Popeye will be waiting for news of two missing players. Announce score as soon as game is played and remember to update numbers for seventh-inning stretch."

CHAPTER 9

The Japanese Airfield

"Lieutenant, what the hell was all that about baseball?"

"McPotts, I think the colonel was telling us there is an old Japanese airfield here and that along with the field, there are some soldiers who stayed behind and are still fighting WWII. I've heard of these diehards, but haven't run into any of them. He says the field is long and will accommodate today's aircraft. The score he is sending will be the coordinates of the old field. The colonel wants the new game to be the basis for our reporting in with the results of our recon, and the seventh-inning stretch will be the continued reports of our progress.

"McPotts, you and Ourdae head down to the PT. Crank up the two-way and take down the numbers for home plate, and while you're at it, warm up the engines. McPotts, you're the navigation expert, so when you get the numbers, find home plate on the map. Make sure O is brought up to date on the current events."

We'd be heading upriver again as soon as we knew the way to San Jose. It's funny how a tune like that would come to a guy and stick in his head at a time like this.

"From now on, gentlemen, the old Jap field—if we find it—will be referred to as San Jose. On second thought, I'll go down to the boat with you. I would like to wake up O myself and ask him how he sleeps so good with so many out there trying to shorten his life span."

"McPotts, have you got the numbers? How far are we from San Jose?"

"Not far, sir. If they crashed at these coordinates, the noise should have been heard from here, so they must have landed like Toms said. No one around here remembers any loud noises like that."

"McPotts, how in hell could they have landed on an airfield no one can see and that hasn't been used for over twenty years?"

"I don't know, sir, but now we can have a look-see!"

"Ourdae, go back up to the bar and get the crew. We're on our way to San Jose."

"McPotts, give O the numbers. Toms, it looks like your dreams from the shamans were correct. There's an old Japanese airfield where the F-4s supposedly went down. No one here or up and down the river ever heard or said anything. We have to assume they landed somewhere near here.

O yelled over the roar of the engines to Lieutenant Primrose, "Sir, do you see the old dock at eleven o'clock on the port, ?"

"Yes, I see it."

"According to your map genius, from the dock it's about two miles inland to the tarmac, or San Jose as we have named it. McPotts says we're right on, no mistake."

Primrose was beginning to feel the excitement of the mission take over his mind and body. "O, bring her into the dock, and we'll tie up and take a look around."

He turned away from the bridge and addressed the crew as O was idling the PT into the dock. "Listen up, gentlemen! As soon as we tie up, I want Toms and Martin to head down the dock and recon the area. Slipps, you and Champion stay on the guns just in case we have problem. Knight, you and Ourdea follow Toms and Martin, but stay back about fifty yards or so. O, you stay at the helm, keep the engines running, and be ready to cast off; we may need to scat in a hurry. McPotts, you come with me, we'll watch the dock area until the others get back from their recon. You guys don't go too far into the jungle, just enough to be sure we're not going to get attacked anytime soon. When it gets dark, we'll hump our way inland to find the old airfield, if it actually exists, and then we'll be able to find out what the hell is going on here."

Primrose sat at the end of the dock watching the Mekong flow towards its eventual dumping into the delta. It looked like any river in the U.S., but it was unusually quiet, with little traffic, which wasn't a good sign, considering the Mekong was the lifeblood of the whole area.

It was comforting so far not to hear the sound of automatic weapons; he guessed the recon teams hadn't run into anything special. If they came running out of the jungle, it'd be time to find another route to San Jose.

Primrose wondered how many Japanese soldiers were still around who didn't believe WWII was over. They could still be trying to protect the field, and with the war ending some twenty years ago, he called that dedication. He was glad the U.S. didn't have to take the Japanese homeland island by island to end WWII. There would have been devastating losses on both sides.

The sounds of footsteps brought Primrose back to the present. He was surprised to see Toms approaching, because he usually couldn't be heard under any circumstances. "Sir, all secure on our perimeter."

"Thanks, Toms, but if everything is secure, where are Knight and Ourdae? They were behind you for backup! How did you return without running into them?"

"We never saw them, Lieutenant. Jesus! I hope they didn't get lost. It's thick-ass shit in there. I guess we could have missed them somehow!"

"Knight! Knight!"

"What the hell, Ourdae, don't yell, we may not be alone here!"

"Knight, did you see Toms and Martin just a second ago?"

"Yeah, they were right in front of us. So what?"

"If that's true, who is that between us and them?" asked Ourdae.

Knight squinted but still had trouble seeing the figure in the thick jungle foliage. "Damn, I don't know. He's just sitting there watching right now, and he doesn't know we're behind him. We could grab him, no problem! What do you think, Ourdea?"

Ourdea was perplexed by the question, and answered, "Hell, I don't know. You're the fucking Marine grunt, not me! Look at the funny-looking cover he has on. You don't suppose he's one of those Japs who refuses to believe WWII is over, do you?"

Knight was still too green in the bush and didn't know what course of action to take. His former MOS didn't qualify him to make the decisions required in combat. "Shit, who knows? Let's watch him for a while and see what he's up to. We can't follow him if he heads into the jungle; we'd get lost for sure. Whoever he is, he didn't engage Toms and Martin. That means he's just scouting. Look, he's heading in the direction of the dock. We'll follow, and if he gets to close, we'll bag him."

"Knight, if that happens we need to capture him alive. He may have information on San Jose. On the other hand, if he's been here over twenty years, I doubt he'll tell us shit. From what I hear from the old salt Marines about these Japs, death would be his option, before uttering a word."

"Damn, Ourdae, he's raising his rifle. Do we shoot him or grab him?"

"Knight, lets make some noise and scare him off. I'll run towards him, and if he doesn't run, you shoot him."

"Wait, Ourdae—shit, there he goes. He's already heard you. We've lost Toms and Martin. We'd better get back to the dock. The Lieutenant will want to know about this pronto."

Lieutenant Primrose was fit to be tied when Knight and Ourdae showed up out of the blue. "Just where in the hell have you two shit-birds been?"

Knight spoke up in their defense, "Lieutenant, we were following Toms and Martin like you said when a third party shows up and gets in the act. He was following the dynamic duo, so we tagged along. He might be one of the Nips still fighting WWII. He had one of those funny peaked hats for a cover. We couldn't grab him without a gunfight, so we decided to scare him off.

"Toms and Martin had disappeared, so when he raised his rifle Ourdae made some noise. He didn't even turn to see where the noise came from: he just disappeared into the jungle like a ghost. We wouldn't have a prayer tracking him in the dense jungle."

Primrose knew that being in command would require some deep thinking and sudden decisions, but this one was a no-brainer. He would ask the colonel to call Heto the tracker from Okinawa. Maybe Heto could find a couple of these holdouts and convince them to give it up and surrender. Who knows, they-could be useful to the team.

He gathered the troops around and said, "Toms, you take the point, and Martin, you bring up our six. Knight, you stay with me and carry the radio—and don't start sniveling, just get the radio"

"Yes sir."

"Ourdea, you follow Knight. Slipps, you and Champion stay with O and the PT. If we find any-thing that requires your special talent, we'll give you a heads-up.

"McPotts, you stick with Toms, but not to close. Make sure he's on the right heading."

As the daylight ebbed away, the night took over the thick jungle. It was black as the inside of a tomb as the team made their way into the thickest jungle any of them had ever seen. Lucky for them Toms could see in the dark, as he lead the way.

After what seemed like forever, they'd made their way about a mile when word was passed up from Martin that someone was following the column. Primrose turned to Knight, "It could be the same guy you saw earlier."

He sent word up to Toms to halt the march, and went back to their six to chat with Martin.

"Martin, if the trailer doesn't bother us, leave him be. If he's one of the soldiers left over from WWII, it would be a shame to kill him after he's lasted this long. Maybe when we get Heto over here, he can talk them into surrendering. We could get them out of the jungle and back home to Japan.'

"Yes sir, that's all well and good, but it gives me the willies to have him on my ass. I could have taken him out a couple of times. He's a little careless—maybe he wants to end it!"

"That's not up to us, Martin. Leave him be, as long as he just follows."

Primrose headed back to the front of the column, hoping the colonel would not waste any time getting Heto. Catching up with McPotts, he asked, "McPotts, how close are we to our objective?"

"I'm sure Toms is already there. We need to start crawling real soon, sir."

Primrose told everyone to hold tight, and he made his way up to Toms at the head of the column. "Toms, find the perimeter of the airfield and then come back for the team. We'll spread out and become invisible until you come back for us."

On his way back to the team, he decided to dub their trailer 'Skoshi.' He hoped that Skoshi would survive to return to his homeland. If he kept his distance, and didn't make any menacing moves, Martin would leave him be.

It was a good hour before Toms crawled up to Primrose and Knight, tapping his rifle to keep from getting friendly fire. He smiled and said, "I could have killed you both, but I felt generous today and allowed you white eyes to see another day."

"Can the shit, Toms. Where are we?"

"Good news, Lieutenant. The old field does exist, and its directly to our front. We can survey the place before daylight. There is something strange about the profile of the airfield. I can't put my finger on it, but there is something strange about the layout."

Primrose passed the word to crawl forward and keep within arms reach of each other. They were within spitting distance of the tarmac before long, with Skoshi in tow on their six. The jungle abruptly ended and the runway presented itself. The landing strip was well-maintained, groomed like a castle garden. Primrose held up the crew and spread the word to settle in for the night. They'd get a good look when dawn exposed the old field. He didn't want to stumble into anything unforeseen and give away their presence. He sent Toms back to check on their newfound backdoor buddy.

Toms, after checking out Skoshi, said to Primrose, "Sir, he is chaperoning our team and has no clue we know about his presence. I can gather him in and not kill him, if you want."

"No, we don't need a prisoner to take care of, but if he interferes with the mission, we'll have to take him out. It would be better if we can wait for Heto and let him try and talk the guy into giving up. Can you imagine the back pay he and however many others there are have waiting. Jesus, twenty years plus years of coin coming. When we get things figured out here, I'll asked the colonel to send for Heto. I think he'd welcome the opportunity to talk these guys into going home. With his connections, Heto could be here in no time, piece of cake! Right?"

CHAPTER 10

Toms

Toms crawled up to Primrose and said, "Lieutenant, I would like an up-close look at the field. Sir, I would like to recon the field while it's dark. No one will ever know I was in the area."

"Toms, can you keep your knife in its scabbard and not do any collecting?"

"Yes sir, I'll just observe, no games."

"Okay, be back at sunup!"

"Yes sir."

With the lieutenants blessing, he couldn't wait to use his Indian heritage to explore the Japanese airfield. He loved the challenge to be the only one who knew he was there. It was darker than the inside of a sweat lodge on the reservation with the fire burned out. Toms, the greatest brave of all time, was in his element.

He crawled up to the tarmac and began his recon, hoping to circle the whole area and find the hangars and HQ buildings. To his surprise, there were no guards visible. Hell, he could have walked down the fucking runway and not crawled through the heavy-ass jungle. He spoke too soon—there was a roving patrol that jumped out of nowhere. He would just watch them and time their routine. They were not very observant, just yakking back and forth, smoking, and driving their jeep down the middle of the black-top like they were cruising the boulevard back home. The jeep looked as old as the field.

The jeep must have come out of a hangar or some other camouflaged building. The whole facility was camouflaged to the max and surely invisible from the air or ground—even in daylight.

Unless a person walked right up to the runway, you couldn't see it, and the buildings could only be seen because of the shadows casting down onto the tarmac. The camouflage work was outstanding. The guards knew the place was undetectable, hence their lack of observant security.

He kept reminding himself, *Just observe Toms, just observe. Just one little peek and I would hat out of there.* He crawled up to the closest hangar, found a wooden hatch covering a small side window and pulled it aside just enough to get a quick look. Sitting at a table were four Russian soldiers playing cards. The team had stepped into heap big buffalo dung. Toms, using the better part of valor, retreated and headed back to the jungle. He wanted to be there before daylight, and inform Primrose there were some unusual personnel manning the field.

Lieutenant Primrose had concerns about being discovered by accident and whispered to Martin, "Pass the word we're heading back to the dock. I don't want to be discovered here. We'll return with the dawn. One of these dumbasses might stumble onto us. When you have everyone on their way, you stay and wait for Toms."

"Aye, aye sir."

Primrose kept an eye for Toms until Martin gave him the thumbs up.

Toms found the return easier than finding the tarmac. The team should be just to his front. He was trying to remember the password and whispered "Watchdog, Watchdog, this is Hunter!"

"Okay, Toms, I hear you, but I can't see you. You have to stop this sneaky shit. You scared the bejesus out of me," said Martin. "And you say Watchdog, and I counter with Hunter. Can't you ever get that straight?"

"Where's the lieutenant?"

"He and the others have gone back to the dock. You go ahead, and I'll stay here and keep an eye on things."

As Toms approached the dock, he kept thinking the lieutenant wasn't going to be pleased to find out the Russians were one of the unknown players in the dangerous game they were playing.

He could see Knight watching the jungle from the base of a tree near the trail leading to the dock and thought about scaring the crap out of him, but decided he might fire a round and give them away—sure would be fun for the Indian! He said, "Hunter."

"Shit, Toms, you have it backwards. You're supposed to say Watchdog, and I reply Hunter."

"Big deal, Knight. I could've slit your throat, and then you couldn't have said shit! Where's the lieutenant?"

"He's down by the dock."

"Thanks, Knight. Keep your eyes open, before someone opens your neck from ear to ear!"

Toms found Lieutenant Primrose sitting at the beach end of the dock, skipping rocks off the water.

"Sir, you look like Tom Sawyer on the Mississippi."

"Right on time, Toms, what did you find out?"

"How many skips did you get with the last stone?"

"Seven, but my record for tonight is eight."

"Sir, their security is poor, and as you know we can crawl right up to the tarmac. I found the hangars and some of the outbuildings, which need a serious inspection in the light of day. There is one thing you won't like one bit."

"Okay, so I won't like it. What can top the way things are so far?"

"Sir, when I took a quick peek into the hangar, there sat four Russian soldiers playing cards. I didn't have time to check out the rest of the hangars and outbuildings. The window I peered into just revealed a small room, and I couldn't see past the card players into the hangar's open bay. From the short visit I had, the whole airfield is one big camouflage project, invisible from the air or ground.

"There must be some kind of netting put over the runways during the day, so satellite or overflights can't see the layout. They, whoever they are, have gone to a tremendous amount of trouble and expense to hide this place."

"Toms, we're going back for a closer look in an hour or so. Are you up to a return trip?"

"Sir, I would rather rest today and keep my night vision for later; it may come in handy. Sir, remember you're invisible right up to the edge of the runway. Then go up around the north end and over to the opposite side—that's the easiest way to the hangars and outbuildings."

"Thanks, Toms, we'll recon from end to end and then be back in time for some rest and out again with the night—you can lead the way."

"Sir, when I said four Russian soldiers were playing cards—I need to rethink that. The more I think about it, the more I believe one of the soldiers may be

Chinese. The plot is getting a little crowded: NVA, VC, Chinese, and Russians. Damn!"

Lieutenant Primrose knew Toms was a good observer and his descriptions would be accurate, which make the situation international.

"Thanks, Toms; now get some shut-eye."

CHAPTER 11

Airfield

"Ourdae, McPotts, mount up. We're heading for San Jose. O, you keep things under control here. Before we jump off, I need to get in touch with the colonel. Who's on the radio?"

"Slipps, sir."

"Ten-four, I'll get with him—be right back."

When Primrose walked up to the PT, he could see Slipps on the bridge scanning the river with binoculars. "How's the traffic?"

"Not much going on this early, sir."

"I mean radio."

"Oh, not much there either, sir."

"Slipps, I need to get in touch with the colonel, would you get him for me?"

"Yes sir."

Slipps dialed in the frequency and said, "Popeye, this is Sailor, Popeye, this is Sailor. Do you read me?"

"Sailor, this is Popeye."

Slipps handed the microphone to Primrose, who tried to be calm and straightforward with the bad news about the new players, but good news about their finding the damn place—to balance things out.

"Popeye, this is Sailor. We are standing on home plate, game score is to follow, many retired players still about."

He motioned for Slipps to send the coordinates of the dock and airfield via morse code. "Popeye, game has more subs than anticipated, new players from bear and panda. Umpires right on, fly balls didn't bounce off fence. Fans will be watching game today. The team needs player scout from the rock to locate retired players and explain the rules."

"Sailor, this is Popeye, have game score, will locate player scout and send to home plate. Keep inning by inning score updated, out."

"Well, Rhonda, what did you think of the transmission?"

"Colonel, I think the diehard Japs are still in the area, the Russians and Chinese are involved somehow, and the jets made a soft landing. Heto is needed to track the Nips who haven't surrendered. But I don't think Toms would like his precious shamans referred to as umpires, even though they seem to be calling the game."

"Well done, Rhonda. You'd make a good code talker, like the Navajos from WWII—the Nips, as you call them, wouldn't understand a word. Do you have Heto's number?"

"Yeah, Zach gave me his little black book, just in case we needed it. There are a couple of pages torn out!"

"I can assure you, Rhonda, Zachary Taylor Primrose has nothing on his mind but you and the job at hand. Would you please get Heto on the phone if possible?"

"I'm on it already, Colonel. There is a lot of static, but it's ringing. Hold on, we may get through on the first attempt."

Rhonda smiled and said, "Hello, Heto, hold please." She handed the receiver to the colonel. "Heto, this is Colonel Easy, how are things, my friend?"

"Things are fine, Colonel, nice to hear you've been promoted. And how is my friend Zach?"

"Primrose is fine, he left word for me to call you if he needed your assistance. He and the rest of his motley crew are on a special mission, and he needs your help, big time. Would you be interested in making a trip to Cambodia?"

"Sure, Colonel, I'm always willing to help Zach. With the right fee this time—this one wouldn't be on the house like last time. Which reminds me, how is Rhonda?"

"That was Rhonda who called. She is fine and sends her regards and thanks for the help last time. Heto, the pay would be the opportunity to track down some Japanese soldiers who haven't surrendered. They're still fighting WWII and don't believe the war is over. Some may even be from your home island of Okinawa. I'll explain all when you arrive if you decide to help ol' Zach out. So what do you think—you want in?"

"What you're telling me, Colonel, is a little far out, but if it's true, I'm in. It would be an honor to help those old soldiers give it up and return home."

"Heto, go to the Dragonfly Bar and Hotel in Phnom Penh. Rhonda and I will be there. Just ask for the entertainment director."

"I'll be there tomorrow."

"Good. See you then, and thanks. Primrose really needs you on this one!"

McPotts raised his arm for the others to halt. He turned around and crawled back the short distance to Lieutenant Primrose, "Sir, I believe we're looking at the hangars there at twelve o'clock."

"I think you're right. Lead out and head around to the north end of the runway, which should bring us up on the other side like Toms suggested."

"Yes sir. Damn, this tarmac looks just like a rice paddy—some job of camouflage. From the air it looks like any other rice paddy in the Far East. If the jets didn't do a nose dive, they have to be in those hangars over there."

Primrose turned to Martin, "You stay here and keep that sniper rifle trained on the hangars in case we need some long-distance help."

Turning back to McPotts and the rest of the team he ordered, "Ourdae, you and McPotts come with me. Knight, you follow us up to the end of the tarmac and drop off there to cover our six."

Primrose noted, "We're blessed these dumb fucks didn't cut the jungle back, which allows us to crawl right up to the hangars. But on the other hand, Murphy is always hanging out there somewhere waiting to screw things up."

The first hangar they investigated was as empty as a drive-in theater at noon and the second shut up tighter than a drum of oil, but lucky for them McPotts, being so tall, managed to peek through an air-vent and reported, "The two F-4s we're looking for are sitting in the hangar just as clean as the day they catapulted off the carrier. There are about twenty guards standing around, in no particular order. I could barely see the second floor, but it looks like office space.

"The jets don't appear to be carrying much of a payload. Just a couple of items hanging from the wings. We need Slipps to take a look and identify the weapons."

Primrose's mind was going a hundred miles an hour. What the hell had they fallen into? "Anything else of interest, McPotts?"

"Yes sir, you won't like this part. There are three different uniforms guarding the jets: Russian, Chinese, and Koreans!"

"Jesus, Koreans—shit, what the hell are they doing here? Damn, this is getting out of hand. The colonel is going to have a fit. We should come back later and snatch one of these fuckers and find out what the hell is going on. Belay that, let's think this out! The jets are here intact, the weapon or weapons are still attached, and there is a multi-force guarding the packages. They don't seem to be in a hurry to make a move, and the jet drivers are nowhere in sight. If we can locate them, we could possibly fly the jets out of here. That's our next move—find the pilots.

"Let's keep snooping around and hope they've not sent the pilots to another facility. Where do you suppose they're holding the pilots, Ourdea?"

"Sir, everything around here has over twenty years of jungle rot, the only thing well maintained is the tarmac. They would probably be held in the most secure building on the field. We can start at the shack next to the hangar."

"Okay, Ourdae, let's do it."

After an extended search, they hadn't found the pilots. There was one building left to investigate, and Primrose hoped they were there.

"Ourdae, this is it, the last building. If the pilots are still here, they have to be in there. You know, we've been here a long time and pretty lucky so far.

90

I think we'll wait until tonight and have Toms and Martin take a peek at this building. It has the most security, so it's probably the one. If we wait until dark, we may be able to sneak up and have a little powwow with pilots and get a handle on the situation.

"There are a lot of questions to be answered, like why did the pilots land here, how did they know where this old field was, and who gave them the coordinates and the orders to do so? Two U.S. fighter pilots, one Navy and one Marine, just didn't take off from a carrier with a couple of super-advanced F-4s, fly them to a foreign country, and disappear by mistake. There is something wrong with this picture. These pilots wouldn't do this without orders from very high up the food chain. Getting to one of these guys is a high priority.

"McPotts, you stay here, but a little farther back in the jungle. Keep an eye out for any movement from the shack. If the pilots are in there and they move before dark, we need to know.

"When we return tonight, we'll look for you right here. If you have to move, don't go far. With this heavy jungle, we won't be able to find you. You'll have to watch for us."

"Yes sir, same passwords?"

"Yes, you'll be Watchdog, and the counter will be Hunter. Be alert. We'll see you tonight, McPotts.

As McPotts stood in the jungle his thoughts wandered: *This is a pretty sight. Here I am in a hostile country, all alone, no back up, no radio, and facing soldiers from three different countries, all of whom would gladly cut my throat in a second. I should have stayed in the Navy. Jesus, how do I do it? This jungle stuff has nothing to do with the art of barroom brawling—this has real Marine shit written all over it. Even in this thick jungle, I don't feel concealed. If those little brown guys see me, I'm dead meat. Like Toms would say, "You tall white-eyes stick out like black cockroach on white rice." I'll take a good ol' aircraft carrier anytime over this grunt cloak-and-dagger caca. McPotts, you must have lost your fucking mind agreeing to this bullshit—won't you ever learn? Come on, darkness. Next time I see Primrose, lieutenant or not, I'm going to wring his scrawny little neck for getting me into this sheep-dip.*

McPotts shook his head to clear out the negative thinking just in time to see the F-4 drivers being marched from the shack towards the hangar where their former rides were stowed. He observed they didn't look any the worse for wear, and they weren't being marched, more like just casually walking. Maybe the bad guys aren't fucking with them too much because they need them to fly or train others on the F-4s.

McPotts was wishing for the darkness to slip over the jungle, because he felt like a redwood standing in an acre of sagebrush. It was not comforting. He noted the pilots walked right into the stowed jet hangar. If they stayed there until the cavalry arrived, it would be difficult to contact them. With any luck they would take them back to the temporary hoos-gow, where they could possibly make contact.

His mind wandered again: *Wish I had a radio! Sit tight, McPotts, be a good Marine. God, I can't believe I said that. Jungle fever must be setting in. I don't like this Marine grunt, jungle- humping shit!*

CHAPTER 12

Second Recon

"O, crank up the radio. I need to get in touch with the colonel," said Primrose. "We have a major SNAFU here."

"Yes sir."

The radio cracked and popped but started to smooth out as the sun dwindled away into the jungle, the vestiges of light bouncing off the river, blinding unprotected eyes.

"Popeye, this is Sailor. Popeye, this is Sailor."

"This is Popeye, hello Sailor."

"Sir, it sounds like Rhonda."

"Damn, I need the colonel."

"Sailor needs Popeye, over."

"Popeye working on baseball scout. Suggest you try American League office."

"The colonel must be at the embassy, sir. "They monitor us twenty-four hours a day. We can contact them, no sweat."

"Bring them up and find a woman named Cleo. She has been helping us, and maybe she can find the colonel for us."

"Lieutenant, the embassy guy has Cleo on the horn."

O handed the phone to Primrose, who took a deep breath and said, "Cleo, Sailor needs Popeye from the Dragonfly."

"Ten-four, Sailor. Popeye present at league office."

"Sailor, this is Popeye."

"Popeye, we have news of ball game. Two fly balls landed in fair ground, not sure about batters. Balls okay to stay in game. Will know about batters in late innings. Home team not very good. Visiting team will require manager to make player change and bring in scout to look for retired players."

"We read you, Sailor. Manager will arrive with scout."

O was still not up to speed on the code talk and said to Primrose, "Lieutenant, I hope the colonel understood all that gibberish!"

"He did, O. And now, how long will it take us to get back to the bar and use the landline?"

"Not long, now that we know where we are and where we're going."

"Good. We'll need to go back and use the landline when the colonel gets here with Heto."

Primrose gathered the troops together. "Gentlemen, it's time to head back to San Jose. Toms, are your eyes in the best shape ever? Are you ready?"

"Yes sir."

"Slipps, you'll go along with us and identify the weapons or whatever is hanging from the F-4s. Martin, you and Toms lead out. Knight, you bring up our six. O, you and Champion stay with the boat. I don't suppose I need to tell Skoshi what to do! Maybe we can keep him alive until Heto talks him in from the cold."

Primrose noticed that each trip was getting easier. They were leaving a nice trail that could be seen by any dumbass who happened along. It was the team's sincere desire that Murphy didn't lead one of the bad guys across their trail.

When they were getting close to the tarmac, Toms came crawling back to guide them the rest of the way, and he was cussing up a storm. "That fucking McPotts is sticking out like a cigar store Indian. I could see him twenty yards away. He should have stayed in the Navy. Jesus, what a dumbshit."

Primrose was suppressing a grin when he asked, "Did you scare the hell out of him?"

"No sir, I didn't want him to start shooting and give us away. Maybe the lieutenant should take his weapons; he could be dangerous to the our side—fucking swabby! He wasn't where he was supposed to be. Daddy longlegs was nearer the outbuilding next to the hangar."

"Okay, Toms, let's get with him and find out what the hell is going on. I'll crawl up first."

Primrose crawled up as close as he dared without startling McPotts. He whispered, "Watchdog, this is Hunter."

McPotts never flinched. "Lieutenant, you know damn well who I am. You ever seen one of these little brown guys over the height of a stump?"

"Nice to see you are alert. Toms says he was here a little while ago and could've cut your throat, no problem."

"Toms is full of shit. He's the only Indian I know who lies every time his lips move."

"Can it, McPotts. Do we have pilots or not?"

"Yes sir, they're in the last shack, like we thought. The bad guys moved them to the hangar where the F-4s are and then back just after dark. They don't act like prisoners, but I hope they are. I don't want to believe they would have landed here of their own free will!"

Primrose turned to Toms and Martin, "You guys crawl up to the shack and check it out, and see if there is a way to get the attention of one of the jet drivers."

Toms responded, "Yes sir. And McPotts, you owe me one for not cutting your swabby-ass throat."

McPotts replied, "Up yours, Toms, you couldn't reach my throat with a stepladder."

Toms could barely balance Martin on his shoulders as he whispered, "Can you see them?"

"Yes, it looks like this is the bunkhouse—they're sitting around reading. No one inside but the two pilots."

Toms was squirming around trying not to drop Martin. "Hurry it up, you're killing my shoulders and neck. Jesus, Martin, stand still! Damn! Is there any way to get their attention? We really need to have a talk with one of them, you know, like right away."

"Quiet, Toms! A Russian just came through the front hatch carrying a bunch of books, and he speaks English! They're talking; everyone is smiling. Hang on, he's leaving. I saw a guard in front when he opened the door. I'm guessing their confinement isn't with their consent. I'm glad to know that. I didn't want to believe they'd sold out.

"The Marine captain is looking up at me, and he has a real dumb look on his face. I don't think he believes what his eyes are telling him. He's walking over to the window, still looking really dumbfounded. The window is sliding open. Cool—it'll open far enough to crawl through.

"Hey, Captain, how's tricks?"

"Jesus, what the hell! Who the fuck are you?"

"Its your lucky day, pal, Martin here, and Toms is below. I'm standing on his shoulders.

"We're from the Scout Sniper Platoon here to save your candy-asses. Wing wipers seem to have their butts in a sling all the time. Good thing for you fellows we stay on standby for just such an occasion as this."

"Cut the shit, Martin, let's get on with it."

"Okay, Toms, lighten up!"

Martin spoke very softly to the captain. "Can you crawl out the window? Lieutenant Primrose wants to talk with you about what the hell is going on here."

The captain was more than a little put out by what he thought was rude behavior by the grunt in the window, "What's your name again?"

"Martin."

"Martin, I think you should remember you're speaking to an officer of the United States Marine Corps, and your respectful attitude should reflect that. I'm not your pal, I'm your superior officer."

"Sir, with all due respect, your ass seems to be in a bind. We're here to help you, and in our line of work a sense of humor is necessary to lighten the load. If we don't get on with the program here, the Marine I'm standing on wouldn't think twice about killing you and me. Now, can you climb out the fucking window or not? Besides that, Captain, I'm not wearing any

100

rank insignia, so it's a guess on your part that you outrank me!"

"Martin, we have lights out here at 2300. I could climb out at that time to meet with the lieutenant. As you can see, we're loosely watched here. These people think they're invisible due to the jungle canopy and their camouflage, which I would have to agree is first class and one hellish place to land.

"Martin, if you're an enlisted grunt, I'll have you up for office hours, due to your disrespectful language."

Toms spoke up loud enough for the captain to hear him, "Martin, I'm done with this shit, either bring that asshole with us now or shove him back into the building."

The captain was not pleased with the remarks by the Marine he couldn't see. "Who the hell was that?"

Martin, just said, "We have to go, Captain. I'll pass the word along to the lieutenant, and we'll be back at 2300. I would recommend, sir, that you pay close attention to the lieutenant. He is your ticket out of here, and he is very impatient."

"Martin, I will have your ass for insubordination."

"Be cool, Captain. We are very few, and there is only one boat to get the hell of out of here with. Our goal is not a firefight, just information first, then we'll decide what plan of action to take with you pilots and the F-4s. See you in an hour or so. Semper Fi!"

"I'm coming down, Toms, heads up."

Toms could hardly keep his voice down as he scowled at Martin, "You and that dickhead captain were as close to death as you're ever going to be without dying. We don't have time for debate or a lecture. Jesus, what the hell were you jawing about?"

"The captain did not like my attitude."

Toms had fire in his eyes, "Fuck him, we'll leave him and take the swabby out of this dump. He might be more grateful!"

Primrose didn't expect Martin and Toms back so quickly, and was startled when they crawled up to his position.

"Sir, the F-4 drivers are in there all right. I spoke to an ungrateful smart-ass Marine captain. He agreed to climb out the window for a meeting at lights out, which is 2300. I believe he thought I was a ghost at first, but he settled down after we talked. He's like all fighter pilots—arrogant assholes. He said he was going to have me up for office hours because of my attitude."

"Thanks, Martin, good job. Toms, take Slipps over to the F-4 hangar and find a way to get a good look at the jets and their cargo before they douse the lights."

"Yes sir, we're on our way. Sir, if you decide to shoot the Marine pilot, I volunteer"

CHAPTER 13

The F-4 Hangar

Toms and Slipps crawled up to the F-4 hangar and were amazed at the lack of security. Toms whispered, "These blackout drapes are just about useless. Good thing for us, huh, Slipps?"

"Hell yeah, we can see the jets just fine. I don't understand these people: there are twenty or so guards inside the hangar and only a couple outside, and then only one at the front entrance. What are we missing here? The thick-ass jungle hides us as well as it does them—chalk one up for the good guys! Toms, you see the rockets hanging from the F-4s?"

"Yeah, so what? What the fuck is all the fuss? There are two F-4s with rockets—big deal!"

Slipps looked over at Toms with the attitude of a teacher dealing with a slow student and remarked, "Lieutenant Primrose is going to shit when I tell him what we're looking at. As a matter of fact, we may have to get Ourdea to revive him from the shock. I can hardly believe my eyes!"

"Okay, okay, Slipps, just spit it out. Jesus!"

Slipps, wanting to pull Toms's chain, took a long time explaining what was attached to the fighter's wings. "What we're looking at isn't just a couple of simple F-4s. Just for your information, smart-ass, those things you call no-big-deal F-4s have Genie rockets on them."

"So what again! A rocket is a rocket. Another big fucking deal. Come on, Slipps. Quit stalling and share your precious knowledge of rocketry."

"Okay, asshole, how's this? The rockets are AIR-2A, more commonly known as the Genie rocket. It's an air-to-air, 1.5 kiloton, nuclear-armed delivery system. Why the F-4s are armed with the Genies is really a mystery. They are usually mounted on Convair F-106s and McDonnell Douglas CF-101 Voodoos. There is some world class shit going on here, and it doesn't look good for the two F-4 drivers.

"What the hell are they doing delivering nuclear weapons to the Russians, Chinese, and Koreans? What's the matter, Toms? You look a little peaked."

Toms looked away from the hangar and the nukes and whispered, "The shamans warned me in a vision about this, but I just assumed it was regular stuff, not nuclear. This is the second nuclear problem for us! Come on, Slipps, let's get back and let Primrose know about the turn of events. Jesus, can't anything be normal once in a while? You believe this? Here we go again with the nuclear crap."

"Settle down, Toms. The rockets are hanging from the F-4s. It's not like the last time, when we had to carry the hot suff around by hand. What we'll do is capture the airfield, fire up the jets, and send them on their way back to the carrier—piece of cake."

"Slipps, we can't do squat until we talk to the F-4 drivers and find out if the jets can even fly. They may not be able to wing their way anywhere. And why have they been sitting for so long? They haven't taken advantage of the situation; they've wasted seventy-two hours. If the bad guys wanted the technology from the jets or the rockets, it should have been accomplished by now. I'm sure they have people who could have flown these birds out long ago.

"On top of that, if the pilots were a problem, they could have dropped the rockets down and hauled them out by truck. What's the fucking hang-up?"

Toms slipped into the darkness of the thick foliage and spoke as softly as he could, "Shit, here comes a couple of those Russians. Get down, Slipps!"

Slipps turned towards the sound of Toms voice. "Too late, Toms; the asshole is looking right at me. Stay where you are—when he gets up close, I'll back in towards you and you can collect another trophy. You take number one and leave number two to me."

Toms grabbed the first Russian and knocked him out cold to the surprise of Slipps, who figured he would slit his throat.

The second Russian became a handful for Slipps. He didn't cooperate like the first one for Toms. During the struggle, Toms clipped the Russian from behind, saving Slipps from a sure-fire week of embarrassment, for being snookered in front of witnesses.

Slipps was thinking, *Shit, now I have to kiss the fucking Indian's ass for a month, having to hear every minute how he saved me from certain death. Shit!*

Slipps laid the Russian next to the one Toms had cold-cocked and said, "Couple of privates—lucky for us. But why didn't you kill them?"

Toms smiled and remarked, "I just wanted to show my white-eyed friend my skills in close order combat. I can see you need some close-up and personal instructions, and I thought the lieutenant might want to interrogate them. It's his decision to kill these fucks, not ours."

"Nice thought, Toms, but now we have to drag them back with us, and they ain't small."

"No, Slipps, we're going to gag the Russkies and tie them to a tree. We'll let Primrose decide what to do with them."

"Okay, Toms. Let's do it and hope these guys were going to take a whizz and not relieve a guard post."

Martin kept checking his watch, and at exactly 2300, he turned to Lieutenant Primrose and said, "It's time. There go the lights. The captain should be coming out of the window anytime now. Should I go help him?"

Primrose was a little irritated with Martin's attitude with the pilot and ordered firmly, "No shit, Martin. Jesus, what the fuck do you think we're doing here? Get your ass down there and lead him back here."

"Yes sir, but he's a real ass, sir."

"Get on with it, Martin."

"Yes sir."

Primrose could see the Marine aviator slide out the window, drop down, and land on Martin, who managed to break the captain's fall. With the captain's input they could get down to what the hell was going on here. If the captain was such a prick as Martin thought, he might be a problem, thinking his rank would put him in charge of the mission. He'd not been in a situation where he'd had to tell a superior officer to take a back seat.

About the time the captain fell out of the window, Primrose could see Slipps and Toms fighting their way through the thick jungle towards his position. They dropped down beside him, and Toms reported, "Lieutenant, we have two Russian privates gagged and tied to a tree near the F-4 hangar. We didn't know if we should kill them or not and decided it was your call, sir."

"Okay, Toms, what happened?"

"Just a fluke, sir. They spotted Slipps when he was moving away from the hangar."

"Damn, Toms, this could put us into extra innings. Murphy is always present. Were they on guard duty, relieving someone, or taking a break?"

"Sir, we don't know, but they were armed with pistols, not rifles."

"Good, maybe they won't be missed until morning. Soon as we finish with the pilots, we'll head back and deal with the Russkies."

"Sir, about the two jets!"

"Tell me about them when we finish with the pilots, Toms."

"Sir, you better have Ourdea on standby when Slipps tells you what we saw."

"The jets can wait, Toms. Here comes Martin with the F-4 driver."

Primrose greeted the Marine pilot, "Hello, Captain, my name is Lieutenant Primrose. My team and I were sent in here to find the remains of two F-4s, destroy what's left of them and bring back the bodies. We didn't expect to find two planes intact, let alone two walking, talking, breathing F-4 drivers.

"My ears are open for your story! You people have half the Navy and Marine Corps brass in some tight ass shorts. As limited as they were with the information on this little boondoggle, it still got around. So what's up, Captain?"

"Lieutenant Primrose, we have a strange tale to tell indeed! I'll begin at the top, which started three days ago. My name is Captain Mann, and my handle is Fuzzball. I won't go into how that came about."

Martin grabbed his crotch and made obscene gestures at the captain.

Primrose ordered, "Martin, can the antics."

Martin could see the challenge in the captain's eyes. A look that meant there was a future between them. That pleased Martin, who would enjoy having a go at the arrogant ass.

"Yes sir."

"Lieutenant Commander Goots is the Navy driver, and his handle is Lockjaw. We were down in the ready room when admiral Dimflipper, requested our presence to his quarters. Naturally, we headed right up to the ivory tower. Arriving just before us were the weapons and flight officers. The admiral appeared to be a bit disheveled as he told us to be seated, but who are we to question an admiral, especially this one? Admiral Dimflipper is the ranking officer in this part of the world, let alone Yankee Station.

"He began with a pat on the back for the jobs we're doing and what a pleasure it was to have such good men under his command. You know, the common atta-boy shit, handed out just before you get your ass reamed.

"But then he got real serious and reminded us that anything heard in his quarters would be considered top secret, like the death sentence if there were any leaks! He said he had orders for us to do a super-secret mission, and that only the people present would know the mission details. In the course of their duties others might wonder about it, but they wouldn't be privy, period.

"The more the admiral talked, the bigger our eyes got. The first thing he told us was that we were to fly into Cambodia to the coordinates that would be provided. Only one driver to each fighter, leaving room for another body. Our objective was to pick up two downed pilots who had information on a target he wanted eliminated. The two pilots were wandering around the jungle after they had escaped their captors, only to be caught again. The black ops guys traded some important information and a lot of gold to the Cambodians for their release. The pilots were supposed to have some info on the location of a special NVA camp stockpiled with weapons, ammo, fresh troops, and high-ranking officers. The admiral said our mission would be to eliminate the target. So far so good, right? Well, the blockbuster is next! Admiral Dimflipper ordered the weapons officer to mount Genie rockets on the F-4s."

Lieutenant Primrose remarked, "So what? You load rockets all the time."

"Lieutenant, we're talking a major escalation of the war."

Slipps stepped in, "How the hell could you allow your planes to be used like that if you had the slightest doubt about the admiral's fitness?"

"Slipps, please allow the captain to finish," said Primrose.

"Yes, sir, but you're going to need Ourdae and some smelling salts."

Primrose looked away from Slipps and addressed the captain, "Go on, Captain."

"Lieutenant, the Genie rocket is a 1.5K air-to-air nuclear weapon."

"Jesus Christ! What the fuck is going on here, Captain?"

"The admiral wanted us to drop the nukes on the targets provided by the two captured pilots. We all stared at each other with questioning looks. What did he just say? Then he says we may shorten the war or even end it. We didn't want to be the first ones to drop a nuclear weapon since 1945, but he told us to get mounted and take off at 0200, so only a few eyes would see our payload.

"Who were we to question the orders of the main man in the Pacific theater? Our only response was to say yes sir and head for the flight deck. What we'd been ordered to do was off the chart, and naturally our first thought was how the hell did we get picked for this hair-brained bullshit?

"The weapons were mounted in record time, the flight deck cleared, and away we go. Goots and I were not willing participants in this mission, but we followed orders, like good soldiers.

"We were told to go below radar when we reported feet dry. This was getting weirder with each new step. Flying on the coordinates given us led us to this old field, and as we approached, this place lighted up like a Christmas tree. They used hundreds of torches to expose the runway. After landing, we expected to pick up a couple of pilots and then skedaddle out of there. NOT. The next thing we saw were Russian, Chinese, and Korean soldiers, fanned out all over the place. They were armed to the teeth, as you might expect of someone receiving nuclear weapons and wanting to protect their investment.

"Now we knew the admiral had set us up, but had no clue why. We were taken from the cockpits to the outbuilding I just came from. They pushed the F-4s into the hangar over there, and the old shack became our home.

"As of now, Lieutenant, we don't have a clue what the hell is going on. They've made no attempt to fly the birds out or truck the weapons. Goots speaks a little Russian from living with his grandparents, and he thinks the Russians are to receive a couple of weapons and the Chinese what's left over. How the Koreans fit into the mix—your guess is as good as mine.

"Now you know as much as we do! Lieutenant Primrose, we think the bad guys are waiting for our side to give up the search for the jets before they move them or the weapons. By the way, how did you find us so quickly?"

Primrose thought about the question for a moment and decided to keep it short. "It's a long story, and

112

most of it you wouldn't believe. It has to do with some Indian shamans, a sniper, a couple of recon troopers, two brown-water sailors, and a PT boat left over from WWII."

Primrose then asked the most important question. "Captain, are the birds flyable?"

"Not both of them, Lieutenant. I made a hard landing. Even with their good maintenance, the runway is not ready for modern aircraft. I'll need a veteran mechanic and some parts to get it up and away. The other bird is fine and has an empty seat, which I would be more than happy to occupy. Lockjaw and I were talking and figured this had to be one of those fucked-up black ops jobs. I don't know if the Genie rockets are the real thing or not; for all I know, they could be dummies. It would be nice to just get in the flyable F-4 and get the hell out of here."

Primrose took a long look at the captain and decided he wasn't such a bad guy but would hold final judgement until he was airborne. "If we have our way Captain, you'll be doing just that as soon as possible. Our CO will be here in the morning, and whatever we do will be up to him. You just sit tight and be patient until we decide how we're going to handle this latest turn of events. We're thin in numbers, but will do everything in our power to get you and the Navy guy in the air and on your way to the nearest friendly landing strip.

"Chances are we'll take the airfield down, and all hands with it. We have some big-time problems out in the jungle besides you and the jets. Martin will help you back through the window before you are missed."

He turned to Martin, "Give the captain a hand. No shenanigans, Martin."

Turning back to the aviator, "We'll be in touch, Captain, and don't give Martin too much shit—he's a seasoned sniper and trigger happy."

"Lieutenant."

"Yeah, Slipps."

"The captain kinda took the fire out of our report on the two birds and their weapons, but he's right about not knowing if they are real or dummies. I'll be able to tell when we get a close-up, hands-on look."

"Okay, Slipps, we'll work on doing that. When Martin gets the wing wiper back to his digs, we'll head back and see about the Russkies."

After Martin returned, Primrose ordered, "Toms, lead the way back to where you deposited the Russkies. Slipps, you bring up our six."

It didn't take long for them to get back to the F-4 hangar area, and Toms, being in the lead, stopped suddenly. The others could hear a loud gasp, "What the hell? Jesus! Lieutenant, both the Russians have had their throats cut from ear to ear!"

Slipps moved around Primrose for a look and said, "We didn't do that. When we left them, they were out cold, not dead."

Primrose looked around and remarked, "Well, they didn't kill each other!"

Toms spoke up again, "Lieutenant, I can't explain it!"

"What's done is done. These guys are going to be missed sooner or later, so let's drag the bodies into the jungle and bury them. How in the hell did they manage to get slit from coast to coast?"

After burying the bodies, they made their way back to the dock. It would be awhile before Colonel Easy and the tracker, Heto, arrived.

"Lieutenant, I have the answer to how the Russians got their necks ventilated. I'll bet a month's pay on it."

"I'll bite—spit it out, McPotts. How did it happen?"

"Sir, I think Skoshi did it. He's still at war with the Russians, Chinese, and Koreans, right? He has kept out of sight, and we don't know what he's been up to."

Toms put his two cents' worth in. "So what? He thinks he's still at war with us too."

McPotts gave Toms an evil look and replied, "Do you have another explanation, Toms?"

Primrose stepped between the two and said, "Okay, McPotts. "If I buy what you say, why hasn't he bothered us?"

"I can't answer that, Lieutenant, except that we appear to be at war with the same people he is, and he can see that. We set them up, and Skoshi finishes the job."

Primrose replied, "That's enough for tonight, guys. Let's get some sack time."

CHAPTER 14

The Korean Connection

As the light was finding its way through the jungle canopy and burning off the mist from the Mekong, the colonel and Heto could be heard making their way upriver. Lieutenant Primrose saw them burst through the mist in a rented longboat. The longboat driver docked the boat with the skill acquired from many years of plying his trade on the huge river.

Primrose greeted his CO. "Welcome aboard, Colonel. Hello, Heto, glad you could make it."

Colonel Easy was all business. "Lieutenant Primrose, tell me you have everything under control here, and we can terminate this mission and go home!"

Primrose hesitated a bit, not wanting to tell the colonel the SNAFU that was at hand. "Sir, I hate to say it, but you won't like what I have to report. You might not even fucking believe it."

"Primrose, every time you report to me, it's more of that you-won't-believe-it shit. So give me a try."

The lieutenant went through the whole story, and then he went over it again because the colonel didn't believe what he'd said the first go around. The colonel just sat there and stared at him like he was in a trance. Then all of a sudden, his face and eyes lit up, and a smile crossed his face. He said, "Finally, it all makes sense, Primrose. The Koreans are the key! Toms, you and Knight come with me, we're going back to the waterfront bar, and use the landline there. It's as secure as you can get on the Mekong, right, Knight?"

"Yes sir, that's where the lieutenant made his last call from."

"Okay, Knight, let's go. Primrose, put everything on hold until we get back. I have some serious shit to put to Division. Fill Heto in on the mission you have in mind for him."

"Yes sir."

As the colonel's longboat shoved off downriver, Primrose turned his attention to Heto and the mission he thought Heto would love to take on.

"Heto, how are you my friend?"

"Fine, Zach, and you?"

"I'm good, and the mission we spoke about is real. You're aware there are some Japanese soldiers from WWII who haven't surrendered?"

Heto smiled. "Yes, I've heard of them, and your point is?"

"Some of those soldiers are defending this airfield with vigor. We're not sure how many, but they're out there. Would you be interested in trying to talk the diehards in and sending them home alive? There is one you might want to start with. I've named him Skoshi: he shadows every move we make.

"Slipps and Toms captured a couple of Russian soldiers and tied them to a tree last night at the airfield to keep them quiet while they were attending to other things. When they returned with me to pick them up, their throats were slit. Slipps thinks Skoshi is the one who knifed the two privates."

"Primrose, I can almost smell Skoshi; the Japanese jungle soldier has a distinct odor about him. I would like to start right away!"

Toms yelled out, "Sir, the waterfront bar is just ahead."

"Knight, do you still have connections at Division," asked Colonel Easy.

"No, not personally, but a major nameed Crowder in crypto is a good friend of Lieutenant Primrose from way back. I could talk to him, and maybe he can help you."

"Knight, when we reach the bar, get on the horn and find the major. I need some sensitive information, and I need it ASAP."

When they coasted into the bar's dock, Colonel Easy said, "Toms, you stay with the boat. Knight and I will go up to the bar. If the boat driver gives you any shit, tie him up. We'll need the boat right after our call to Division."

The colonel didn't find the apperance of the bar reassuring. "Knight, this is the bar McPotts runs, right?"

"Yes sir. It's their home away from home and their northern HQ; hence the good landline. The phone is strictly business only, and I never asked what kind of business. There is a small arsenal up stairs, so I think their business is a little on the shady side."

"No shit, Knight. Well, it takes all kinds to fight a war—just be glad their on our side," remarked the colonel.

Colonel Easy hoped leaving Toms along with the boat didn't backfire. If the guy gave him any shit, it wouldn't be pretty, and they needed his river experience. He followed Knight up to McPott's bar and the landline.

When they entered the bar, all heads turned towards the new-comers. The patrons of the ginmill were a collection of river scum of the lowest kind sitting at the tables and standing at the long bar—each looking to relieve the other of anything of value. False smiles and phoney handshakes were the trademarks of all present.

"Jesus, will you look at this collection," said Colonel Easy, "If you were looking for a crew to rob, steal, and plunder, this is the best recruiting ground in the world. Damn! How does McPotts and his motley crew survive?"

Knight pointed out the mama san standing near the juke box, looking every bit as tough as her customers. "She's McPotts's trusted general foreman."

"Tell her we need to use the private landline."

Along with every eye in the smoky den of thieves, Easy watched Knight walk over and speak to the old woman. He wondered how the hell such a collection of reprobates could get along for more than a few minutes.

Knight returned. "Colonel, she says McPotts told her no one uses that particular phone except Primrose—she won't give it up."

"Knight, tell her it's okay, that I'm McPotts and O's boss. And if that doesn't work, tell her we'll rob her burial grounds and dump the bones in the nearest benjo!"

"Sir, she understands English and isn't smiling, but she says we can use the phone for one hundred Yankee dollars per call."

"Sure, whatever she wants, give her a chit for the money. Where's the phone?"

"It's in the office behind the bar."

"Knight, get Division on the phone and find this Crowder guy."

"Yes sir."

Even with the best installation, the phone system was a comedy of errors, but if one kept trying and refused to give up, connection was possible.

Knight kept plugging away and finally, "Sir, I have Major Crowder." He handed the phone to Colonel Easy.

"Major Crowder, this is Colonel Easy, I'm Lieutenant Primrose's commanding officer. We're on a special mission, and he indicated to me that I could talk to you, man to man, no bullshit!"

"Yes sir, whatever Primrose said, then that's the way it will be. How may I help you Colonel?"

"Major, it's my understanding that you work in the crypto section, right?"

"Yes sir."

"Do you know anything about two F-4s that have come up missing in the last four days?"

"Yes sir."

"Major, our mission has to do with the missing F-4s. I'm sure you know who Admiral Lincoln Taft Dimflipper is?"

"Yes sir."

"He plays a part in our mission, and I need some sensitive information about him.

"Can you provide me a history of his service jacket?"

"I can try, sir."

"Okay. Look through his file and see if he was ever a POW during the Korean War, and if he was, how long and where was he held. Then follow up on his history since Korea. Where his duty stations were, schools, list of fellow POW's, what his security clearance investigation turned up, and finally his medical records, physical and mental."

"Damn, Colonel, are you selling life insurance, or what? All kidding aside, that's a lot of information on the commanding officer of the whole Pacific Fleet. He's the man in this part of the world."

"Believe me, Major, this is an industrial-strength situation we have in our hands. What we learn about the Admiral may save the lives of thousands of military and civilian personnel."

"Okay, Colonel, I'll get back to you as quick as I can. This amount of personal data will require some very inventive methods, and I'll have to step on some highly polished shoes to get it done."

Colonel Easy's voice became deadly serious, "Major Crowder, this may be the most important information you've ever gathered. Please leave the line open; we may not get this good of a connection again. We'll wait—you can't imagine how important this is!

Colonel Easy turned to Knight, "Knight, is Slipps damned sure about the weapons hanging from the two birds?"

"Yes sir. Sir, what's the deal with the admiral?"

"Knight, if the information on the admiral comes back like I think it will, we'll know how this whole affair got legs."

As the colonel and Knight sat at one of the bar's cleaner tables near the back office, Colonel Easy said, "Have you noticed that almost everyone in this sleazy establishment looks like a character in a Bogart movie? That trio of rogues who man our PT boat, are starting a legend here on the river system that may last for decades. How long have we been waiting on the major?"

"About two hours, sir."

When the frustration of waiting was about at its peak, the bar boy who was hanging on the phone, yelled out, "Phone, phone."

Colonel Easy grabbed the receiver. "Hello, Colonel Easy here."

"Hello, Colonel Easy. I have the information you requested, and this is how it plays out. When the admiral was fresh out of the academy, he was flying missions over Korea. On his last sortie, he was shot down and spent sixteen months as a POW. He was confined with two other Naval aviators and a Marine grunt. One of the other pilots is now a captain, and the other is dead. The Marine grunt is a general. The admiral has been to all the appropriate schools for his rank. His fitness reports are excellent, and he's a genius in Naval tactics. The admiral is top drawer all the way, Colonel."

"Major, is there the slightest blotch on his record anywhere, no matter how small—anything that would raise a flag?"

There was a long pause before Major Crowder spoke, "Not that I could find sir, except there is one thing that's a little out of the ordinary. He took leave a few years ago—two to be exact—and was unaccounted for, for a week. It was explained away as a lack of communication. He said he was in Germany doing a genealogy thing on his family."

Colonel Easy's voice gave way to a flash of excitement, "Major, your help has gone beyond my expectations. And Major, when is the best time to catch the commanding general?"

"For his office, the morning is a good time, and in the evening the Officers' Club. He is aboard for the rest of the week, with no inspections, conferences, or parades to attend."

"Thanks again, Major, I'll get back to you."

"Colonel, in reference to my future in the Corps, it would help if you forgot where you found out all the information we just shared!"

"Major, my memory has just taken a vacation. Your future is safe with me. Thanks again."

Easy replaced the receiver and walked back out to the table. He remarked to Knight, "You wanted to know what was going on with the admiral. I believe I can tell you now, with the information we just received from Major Crowder. He may have uncovered where all this cloak-and-dagger shit came from. The Marine on duty with the admiral when I was out on the carrier told me some very interesting things about his behavior. Much of what the Marine said about his state of mind at times matched some of the reports I read about such things from the Korean War and POW's.

"During the Korean War, when the enemy captured our troops, they tried to brainwash them into believing in communism. This was done in different ways, and brainwashing may not fit what was done to the admiral. I rather think he was programmed to act upon seeing or hearing certain words or phrases. When the key word or phrase is heard or seen, the program implanted in his head in the fifties begins, and he starts to perform the task. People who've been programmed like this usually become oblivious to their surroundings, and they focus on what the program says to do.

"I believe Admiral Dimflipper is a communist sleeper, programmed to act at the appropriate time. The admiral doesn't know he's being used."

Colonel Easy was anxious to contact the commanding general, "Knight, what is the best way to contact the general at this hour?"

"Sir, like the major said, the general is probably at the O Club at this hour. I would start there, sir."

"Is there a secure line at the O Club?"

"Yes sir, at the general's table, but the only way it will ring is going through the general's office; they screen all his calls. There is always someone there to answer the phone."

"Okay, Knight, get the general's office on the horn and tell them to patch me through to the O Club. Inform them that I need to speak with the general ASAP, in regard to a serious situation."

The mama san came over and offered the colonel and Knight some chow and drinks. It was her way of apologizing for her rude behavior when they'd first arrived. She had lived through six different invaders of her country and had survived them all by using her wits. Being cooperative was usually a winner. McPotts was smart getting her to watchdog over this scumbag establishment. From her demeanor it was clear she didn't take any shit from anyone and made him a nice profit.

Looking around at the crowd in the joint, they decided she probably had some firepower behind the bar and the knowledge to use it. The tables weren't crowded with suits and ties. The rogue drinking here looked every bit the part of river rats that had plenty of dough to spend.

There was a guy standing behind the bar whose body wouldn't allow any light through the doorway to his back. They figured he was her backup. She had chosen well; he was huge and mean-looking to boot. The three PT rogues, who always lived on the edge, had a nice safety net stretched out here, just in case ol' Murphy pissed on their parade.

"Colonel, the general's office is putting the call through."

Easy took the receiver and after a short delay, he heard, "This is General Fleetside."

Easy inhaled a long, slow breath to fill his body with much needed oxygen. It wasn't every day a lowly grunt Lieutenant Colonel was about to accuse the leader of all forces in the Far East of treason. "General, this is Lieutenant Colonel Easy, and I've some serious business to discuss with the general. It pertains to the missing eagles and the officer who gave them their mission. I don't believe the general is going to be happy with what I have discovered! Before the general stops me in mid-sentence, please hear me out."

"I'm listening, Colonel, and this better be more than just a good story."

"Yes sir. I'll get on with it. Does the general know Admiral Dimflipper?"

"Yes, I know him very well. We attended Staff College and some other schools and duty stations together over the years."

"Sir, did the general know the admiral during the Korean War?"

"Yes, he flew fast movers for our air cover on more than one occasion, and as you well know, it's a pretty sight to see one of those jet jockeys come in real low and dump on the enemy just yards to your front. He was a damn good jet driver. What are you leading up to, Colonel?"

"Sir, if the general will be patient and hear me out, it will all make sense in the end. General, were you aware the admiral was a POW for a considerable length of time?"

"Yes, I'm aware of that fact, Colonel. Colonel, this is not a court room, get to the fucking point—you're not the only person on my agenda!"

"Sir, to get right on point, I think the admiral is a deep-seated Communist sleeper, programmed to react to a certain word or phase and follow through with the instructions given him, visual or auditory. He ordered those jets to take off and land at a predetermined site.

"We've found the F-4s and the drivers in good condition. They're in Cambodia!"

Easy heard a gasp as the general retorted, "Jesus Christ, Colonel! Why wasn't I notified about this?"

"Sir, we just found them, and that's some of the good news. Sir, the F-4s are intact—one needs some repairs after a hard landing; the other is flyable. That's about the end of the good news.

"The insertion team managed to get the Marine pilot out of his confinement and returned without revealing their presence. The pilots have no idea what's going on. They were just following orders.

"General, freeing the pilots and recovering the aircraft are not our biggest problem. We have Russians, Chinese, and Koreans that would have to be eliminated before we make good an escape!"

Easy could hear the general yelling at people in the background as he said, "Wait a minute, Colonel, you're going a little too fast here: slow down and fill in the blanks. We started with two missing jets, and now you're about to start a very sticky international incident and maybe WWIII. Slow down, cover all the bases, quit beating around the bush. Give it all to me. What are you holding back?"

Easy could see the general on the other end of the line about to blow a gasket, thinking about all the diplomacy that would be required to stop the dam from bursting if they killed a bunch of Russians, Chinese, and Koreans—no matter the reason.

"Yes sir, as I was saying, the Russkies, Chinese, and Koreans are involved in this flap up to their scrawny little necks. The real bombshell is the F-4s were not armed with a traditional weapons load. Sir, the jets were equipped with Genie rockets. Is the general familiar with that rocket system, sir?"

"Colonel, I'm a grunt officer. I'm not familiar with all the wing wiper shit. Now get on with the fucking program and stop all this gibberish."

"Sir, the Genie is a 1.5K nuclear air-to-air weapons system, and they are sitting on an old Jap airfield in Cambodia as I said. I believe this has been courtesy of the Korean sleeper program, which is bearing fruit after some fifteen or so years. Sir, the admiral is an unwitting partner in this theft of weapons. It's my belief the admiral was preprogramed to act.

"It all came to me when I learned he'd been a POW in Korea. The Marine on duty with the admiral the night I was ordered to his quarters told me some fascinating and disturbing things about Admiral Dimflipper's behavior. If the general would call the Marine ashore, he could fill in the blanks. I know these accusations are wild, to say the least, but there is more, sir."

"What the fuck could be more than nuclear, Colonel?"

Easy got the feeling the general was going to pounce on some heads at the end of the phone conversation, and was happy to be in Cambodia, and not at Division HQ.

"Sir, according to the Marine pilot, the Koreans sold the jets and weapons to the Russians and Chinese for some big bucks and numerous favors down the road. As I said, none of this could have been possible without the full cooperation of the admiral. The weapons officer and his crew were sworn to silence by the admiral. I believe all this took place while Dimflipper was under the influence of the sleeper program."

There was a long pause on the line when nothing could be heard but the general's heavy breathing.

"Sir, everything is on the table. How does the general want my team to handle this situation?"

The general didn't answer right away. He finally posed a question to a question. "You're on the ground there, Colonel, what do you think would be the best course of action?"

"Sir, number one, we capture the airfield, weapons, and jets—which will require us to eliminate a bunch of the people we talked about earlier, and then fly the good bird out and bring in a Chinook to lift the other out.

The second scenario, we steal the flyable bird, blow the other one up, and scoot out of there. Third scenario, we give the general the coordinates of the Jap airfield, slip away in the night, and the general has a flight of B-52s leave a grease spot where the airfield was. Whatever the order sir, we don't have much time. The Genie rockets could be moved anytime, with or without the F-4s."

The sound of the general's voice yelling at everyone within his grasp was so loud Easy had to hold the headset away from his ear. "Colonel Easy, you've ruined my meal, upset my stomach, and pissed me off big time. If you are one centimeter off on your accusations of Admiral Dimflipper or the authenticity of the Genie rockets, you'll spend the rest of your natural life in the deepest part of Leavenworth, if I don't have you executed first.

"Colonel, do not hang up the phone. You will stand at attention until I get back to you. I may send a planeload of Marines to arrest you and that group of nonconformists you call Marines. I should've had you all committed the last time we had dealings. Don't move a muscle, I'll be right back—shit!"

The general was either using another line to have a fast mover drop a bomb on the team or he believed Easy and was getting his staff up and running to lay out a scenario to cover all their bases.

While Colonel Easy was waiting on the phone, he relaxed a little, knowing the general couldn't see that he wasn't at attention, and vaguely heard Knight, say, "Sounds like the general is really pissed, I could hear him all the way over here."

"That's not all, Knight. he's really going to blow a fuse when he confirms this is all true. At that point I wouldn't want to be in his shoes and have to bring down the ranking military officer in this part of the world!"

As they waited for the general to come back on-line, they could visualize him yelling at everyone within earshot to get this record or that person or what have you, all ASAP. People would be scrambling in every direction, some to hide and others to do his bidding—all in the path of his wrath.

CHAPTER 15

Admiral Dimflipper

General Fleetside ordered his aide, "Major Later, get the *Hornet's* captain on the radio ASAP."

"Yes sir."

Major Later, seeing the general's mood, made quick work of the contact, not wanting the anger to spill on his plate.

"Sir, I have a Captain Krueger from the carrier."

"Captain Krueger, this is General Fleetside, is Admiral Dimflipper still aboard?"

"Yes sir."

"Captain, we have a serious flap going on here, and I need some sensitive information."

"How may I help you, General?"

"You are aware of the missing F-4s?"

"Yes sir. That has become a major problem for me."

"What can you tell me about their mission?"

The captain didn't like the line of questioning, but he didn't have any choice but to engage the general.

"Not much, General. The admiral handled the mission personally, something to do with top secret, his responsibility, period. And he remarked that I should stand down until further notice. I thought it very odd from the beginning.

"The admiral remarked something about taking the heat if the mission failed, and it wouldn't affect my career."

General Fleetside was incredulous. "Rather unusual for a ship's captain not to know everything that goes on aboard his ship, especially something of this magnitude."

"Yes sir, I agree."

Captain Krueger was thinking, *Being a ship's captain is pressure enough. What the hell does this Marine general have to do with my missing F-4s and what business does he have with a fleet admiral? On my next tour, I'll try to avoid being the flagship for any admiral.*

"Captain Krueger, I need to speak with your weapons officer and the crew that was on duty the night the F-4s launched. I would like to speak with the Marine who was on duty with the admiral the same night, I'd like a description of the weapons mounted on the jets. I'm sure the captain can provide me with those personnel and some answers."

"General, I can send you the personnel you have requested, but answers will have to come from them. I can't help you with any information from me personally. The mission was limited to the weapons officer and his crew. The admiral was adamant about that."

General Fleetwood was about to reach into the radio and grab the captain by the short hairs, not believing his excuses. "Captain, I find it hard to believe you don't know what the fuck's happening on your own fucking carrier! Since when did the captain of a ship give up his responsibility of command?"

Captain Krueger was slow to answer, knowing how the general must think he didn't have control of his own ship. "As I said, General, Admiral Dimflipper is the commander-in-chief of the Pacific Forces, and he is also your boss, I might add. If he gave you an order to stand down, I think you would do just that."

"Okay, Captain, you've made your point. Would you put those people on a chopper ASAP?"

"Yes sir, I will do that immediately. Is there anything else I can do for the general?"

"Yes, you can come along with your people. We have some serious shit to discuss about Admiral Dimflipper and the F-4s."

"Yes sir, we'll lift off right away."

Captain Krueger thought, *A ship's captain has a lot of power, but only aboard his vessel and only when the fleet admiral isn't aboard. Heading for the beach will put me out of my element. I wonder what the hell this grunt general is so uptight about? I haven't been to the beach for an ass-chewing since I was a lieutenant junior grade. This has to be some serious shit, and I'm going to find out what the hell this is all about before going ashore.*

Captain Krueger turned to his first officer and said, "Get the weapons officer and the crew who were on duty the night the F-4s took a powder, and while you're at it, get a chopper ready to take everyone to the beach."

The first officer found the lieutenant and said, "Lieutenant."

The weapons officer could tell by the sound of the first officer's voice, something heavy was about to fall on him. "Yes sir."

"The captain wants to see you and the crew who mounted the weapons on the F-4s the night they disappeared. I suggest you get yourself and that crew up there right away. The captain is red-faced, with steam coming out of his ears, and he is about to sever some heads. I recommend you don't leave yourself open on any front. He's on the warpath."

"Sir, do you know the source of his agitation?"

"Yes, there's a Marine general on the beach who is all over the captain about something he didn't share with me."

The weapons officer's face showed signs of distress as he said, "Damn, they must have found the F-4s. Now the shit is really going to hit the fan. I'll get my crew together and get up to officer country. This isn't going to be a pleasant situation for me, the crew, the admiral, or the Marine general. I can see the yardarm being made ready for a hanging. I'm on my way, sir. Oh, by the way, does the admiral know the Marine general?"

"No, Lieutenant, I don't think so. He didn't mention that he did."

"Gunny, I need to see the Marine on duty with the admiral the night the F-4s were launched, right away," ordered the first officer to the Gunnery Sergeant on duty.

"Yes sir, he's down in the mess hall. I can have him up here in no time. Is there anything I can do to help? He is a fine Marine sir, one of the best in the unit. I can't imagine he's done anything that would require a chewing by the captain."

"No, Gunny, this is something the young Marine has to handle when he gets up there. Send him to the captain's cabin, and have him squared away and ready for a ride to the beach."

"Damn, what the hell did he do?"

"Nothing outside of his duties. I can't share the situation with you, Gunny."

"Yes sir, I'll get him on his way."

"Thank you, Gunny."

"Captain, all the people you requested are on the way," reported the first officer.

The captain had calmed down a tad as he retorted, "Thank you. When they report, I don't want to be disturbed for any reason short of another Pearl Harbor, and I want a chopper ready to lift off within the hour."

"Yes sir."

"Captain."

"Yes, Corporal."

"The personnel you requested are outside. The weapons officer, his crew and one Marine."

The corporal stepped outside the captain's cabin and said, "Gentlemen, have a seat, the captain will be with you shortly. If I may be so bold, the captain's mood is to bite someone's head off. I would suggest you pretend this is a confession booth. Please excuse my frankness."

After giving those gathered time to sweat a little, the captain stepped out of his cabin. The corporal on duty sounded out, "Attention on deck."

"As you were, gentlemen. I have gathered you here to get to the bottom of some sensitive activity that happened a few nights ago. I'll expect your full cooperation in the matter. We'll start with the night the F-4s were launched. I'm assuming everyone in my presence is familiar with the event. Lieutenant, you're the senior man here: you're invited to speak first. Please start at the top and share the events with me."

"Sir, I respectfully decline to reveal any details relating to the night in question, and that includes my crew. I can't speak for the Marine, sir."

General Fleetside, upon hearing the officer's refusal to answer his pointed question, blew a gasket. "Lieutenant, I'm going to give you one more opportunity to respond about your knowledge of the events in question before I put you and your crew in irons!"

The weapons officer stood his ground in deference to the admiral's orders. "Sir, I'm following the orders of the admiral. I refuse to reveal the mission."

"Corporal, what do you have to say?" asked the general.

The corporal was nearly as white as a sailor hat, but stood his ground, "Sir, I don't know what went on in the admiral's quarters when the lieutenant was there. I was only present for a moment. I have nothing to add to the scenario."

As he looked over the men, Captain Krueger was thinking: *What the hell is going on here? Are these men close to mutiny? In all my years in the naval service, I've never run into anything even close to this situation. A closed-mouth bunch of sailors and an admiral who is distant, to say the least. Then there's a Marine general ready to eat everyone within range for dinner. The topper is that it has started from my ship, and for now it is out of my control. Damn!*

The general regained his composure and ordered, "Gentlemen, I'm so happy I got you up here and received so much cooperation. I'm so happy about this that someone is going to hang from the yardarm or be keelhauled if I don't get some answers. You people will now do an about-face, head down to the flight deck, and board a waiting chopper. I'm positive there will be some blabbering when we get to the beach. There is a Marine general who outranks me, and he wants to see you badly. Any skin taken from my ass by the general will be taken double from your asses when and if we get back to the ship. You best be thinking how dark Leavenworth is in the winter, spring, summer and fall. You'll be so far down in the bowels of that institution, daylight will be a foreign word. Now move out!"

On the ride to the beach one of the sailors asked the weapons officer, "Lieutenant, we are just ordinary seamen, how do we respond to questions from a Marine general?"

"Sailor, you don't even have to think about it. We will not reveal what was mounted on those birds to anyone. Those orders came from the commanding officer of the Pacific Fleet. How hard is that to understand? The admiral outranks every swinging dick in this part of the world."

"Sir, we will be on the beach with the Marine general dumping on us, and the admiral will be out there on Yankee Station!"

142

"Just keep your mouth shut. I'll do all the talking and answer all the questions. Whatever heat there is, I'll take it—end of story."

"General Fleetside."

The voice startled the Marine general out of his thoughts that he might soon have to bring down the highest-ranking naval officer in the Pacific Theater. After thirty years plus service, with retirement coming quickly, it would not be a pleasant task. The admiral was a good sailor and dedicated to the Navy and his country. Being shot down in a war years ago may have come back to haunt him. Getting this flap squared away ASAP was a no-brainer.

"General Fleetside."

"Yes, Lieutenant."

"General, the troops from the *Hornet* are here."

"Thank you. Please send them in."

"Yes sir."

He opened the door and waved the troops into the general's office, then retreated and closed the door, not wanting to hear the tongue-lashing that was about to take place.

"Gentlemen, stand at ease. Before we go into detail about the flap before us, I will tell you what I know, and then you will fill in the blanks. Everybody, one by one, will step forward and tell me exactly what you know.

Everything needs to see the light of day, and I mean everything, all out in the open. Careers of many men lie in the balance, not to mention the lives of the men in the field who are also involved in this convoluted mess. We have some serious accusations going on here. The brig on your ship is ugly and unpleasant, with enough cells for all of you. Anyone not willing to cooperate will find himself there before his transfer to something worse. I assure you, the next stop will be atrocious! Do I make myself clear?"

The assembled troops looked so young, and they probably didn't have a clue what the hell was going on, but the general had to challenge them to get what he could out of them. Every scrap of information would be helpful in straightening this mess out.

"Gentlemen, I'm looking into the eyes of each and every one of you. That may make you uncomfortable, but this is serious shit. I'm going to bring you up to date first, but before I begin, anything you hear here will stay here when you leave. Nothing will leak from this room, in any shape, manner, or form. A firing squad will be your reward for any loose lips.

"This is what we have at present. There is a Marine recon team out in the field as we speak. The unit has located the missing birds and their drivers in Cambodia. One bird is flyable and the other can be repaired, but that's not the biggest problem at hand. Some of us in this room know what the biggest problem is! Isn't that true, Lieutenant?

"For those of us present who don't know what I'm talking about, I'll fill you in. The F-4s were armed with

144

Genie Rockets by the weapons crew of the lieutenant here. If you're not familiar with the Genie Rocket, it's a 1.5K nuclear air-to-air weapons system."

Captain Krueger couldn't believe what he'd just heard. The color had drained from his face, which then turned red when he looked over at the weapons officer. He gave the lieutenant a look that would have killed a normal person. How could two F-4s leave his ship with nuclear weapons without his knowledge? The lieutenant's loyalty should have been with his ship and captain. Damn the admiral and the weapons officer. "General, I'm dumbfounded."

The general continued, "The recon troops have a mission to accomplish, and they're in position. We need to discuss the best options for them to go with. They're standing by in a deadly hostile environment. I'll start with you, Captain Krueger."

"General, as I said, I'm dumbfounded. I don't know any more than what we talked about on the horn. I don't have anything to add to what has been revealed here, but there is one thing—I'll fill my brig when we get back aboard ship."

"Okay, Captain."

The general turned to the weapons officer, "Lieutenant, it's your opportunity to come clean before I have you locked up for insubordination. I need information to relay to those troops on the ground, poised for an attack. You will tell me everything you know about this fiasco, and what you and your crew have done to help it along."

The lieutenant stood and decided it was time to go against the admiral's orders. "General, me and my crew were following the orders of Admiral Dimpflipper. We were ordered to arm the Genie rockets and mount them on the F-4s. The admiral gave us strict orders to never reveal our mission. He gave us those orders in his cabin the evening the jets were launched. The F-4 drivers were present, and he gave them the coordinates for a mission to pick up two POW pilots who would guide the birds to their respective targets. After launching their payload, they would return to Yankee Station and the *Hornet*.

"The admiral suggested that using the rockets for bombs would shorten the war, maybe even end it, and he added the mission came from the highest authority— meaning the President of the United States. I ordered my crew to do the job, so I'm responsible for their actions as well as mine."

"Thank you lieutenant. Now Corporal, what do you have to add to this gruesome comedy?"

"Sir, could I speak to the General in private?"

"Hell no, Corporal! Didn't you hear me? This informal inquiry will be wide open—wide fucking open. Now get on with it."

"Yes sir. I told the colonel leading the recon team that the admiral had been acting funny. I was present when the admiral was reading a letter, and out of the blue, he went into outer space and wasn't even aware of my presence. This also happened one time when he was on the phone—like he just disappeared from the here and now.

"The recon colonel was suspicious about the admiral's orders from the beginning, and there were two significant times that I was with the admiral when he just went away mentally. Both times there was a common factor, sir.

"The first time, the word *KENO* was typed across the top of a letter he was reading, and the other time, I heard the word on the phone by accident. Both times the admiral went into a trance-like state. The only common denominator being the word *KENO*. Sir, from the military history of the Korean War, it sounds like the admiral was brainwashed or something while a POW."

"Thank you, Corporal. Captain, you and your weapons officer please stand by, the rest of you head over to the slop chute or mess hall. I'll send for you when I need you again. Thanks for your cooperation.

"Captain, I have the recon team on hold, what do you recommend for our best course of action?"

"Sir, we need those rockets back. They are the state of the art in air-to-air nuclear weapons. If allowed to fall into the wrong hands for very long, they can be back-engineered, no problem. In which case we'd have a world-class flap on our hands. The rockets could be sold to any crackpot, tinhorn dictator or terrorist on the planet. We need them back."

"At any cost, Captain?"

"Yes sir, at any cost—they're that important. The Koreans sure picked an opportune time to use their sleeper cell, after so many years."

"Thank you, Captain. Now, Lieutenant, what is your take on the situation? You're the weapons expert, what do you think? Do the rockets work?"

"Sir, the Genies are lethal and will work when launched. They will hit any target aimed at, and I agree with the captain, we need to recover the birds, their drivers, and the rockets. Sir, I had a lot of reservations about arming the F-4s and thought the admiral was acting funny, but who am I, to question the commanding officer of the Pacific Theater?"

"As you can guess, gentlemen, I'm very unhappy with this whole affair being dropped in my lap. Captain, you can pick up your crew and head back to the *Hornet*. Don't keelhaul anyone until you check with me, as a professional courtesy."

"Yes sir."

"I'll be in touch after I get with the Commandant of the Marine Corps or higher to see what the next step will be with the admiral. If he is to be relieved of his command, I'll chopper out and give you the word personally.

"If it comes to that, the Navy should be the one to perform that regrettable duty. I don't envy you the task. And don't forget, it's not the admiral's fault. The docs will have to figure a way to deprogram him. In the meantime, he has to be removed from his position, so his authority can't hurt us."

CHAPTER 16

Skoshi

The recon team had been cooling their heels in the scumbag waterfront bar for some time, and the dregs who hung out there were giving them hungry, threatening looks, like they might have something real stupid going through their pinheads. The mama san smiled at everyone and ran the place with an iron fist, with the giant shadowing her every move. So the beady-eyed little shits just smiled and wished they could take out the Yankees.

Colonel Easy poked Knight to get his attention. "How long has it been?"

"Colonel, its been nearly six hours. They must be having a hard time going against the admiral. Do you know the general well?"

The colonel didn't think about the question for more than a second and said, "From what I know about him, he's a no-nonsense kind of officer. His philosophy is if you can't lead, then follow or get the fuck out of the way. If this war was up to him, it would be over in six months. The general would go into the bush in a second and lead the way to victory."

"Sir, the general of whom you speak is on the line!"

Easy took the receiver, "General, Colonel Easy here."

The general's voice sounded a little sad and excited at the same time to Easy. The burden on him to even think of trying to relieve a fleet admiral must be tremendous. The sweat was starting to bead up on Colonel Easy's forehead, wondering what was in store for his team. The general began, "Colonel, I have only a few things to address. Thank you for figuring out the Korean connection.

"With the current situation becoming clear, I believe you are right, and I agree the admiral is a sleeper project. I'll deal with that. Naturally, the carrier captain and weapons officer recommended we recover the birds, weapons, and drivers intact, at any cost, and I concur. I'm sure you can handle whatever comes up, Colonel."

"Yes sir, General."

"Colonel, you use your best judgment and wherewithal to accomplish your goal. You are on the ground there, and I won't presume to tell you how to proceed. The next thing I want to hear from your end is a couple of F-4s buzzing over my head, giving me a belly roll, to let me know mission accomplished."

"Yes sir, I'll relay that to the wing wipers, sir."

"Get on with it Colonel, and use whatever resources you need. Use my name if it'll help you. I'll back all your play."

"Thank you sir, Semper Fi."

Colonel Easy replaced the receiver and turned to Knight, "They don't want much, just everything intact! Jesus, there's going to be one hell of a gunfight over this shit, and the bad guys aren't going to just throw their hands in the air. Maybe Heto can get the Japs to help us—that would be our ace in the hole.

"I believe things are going to get real sticky. A sticky wicket, as the Brits would say. Let's get back to the longboat.

"Toms will be glad to hear the news, as will Martin; they can add to their collections. Champion won't be pleased—he would rather trigger one of the Genies, being the sick puppy he is. Slipps will be a happy camper, being able to get a close-up, hands-on look at the weapons."

When they got back down to the dock, the Colonel ordered Toms, "Get us back upriver. We've been given the green light to engage and start the recovery. I'll explain on the way."

Toms, the ultimate warrior, as usual had only one response to the call to arms. "Sounds good to me, Colonel. It's time for some real action. It's been a while since we've heard the sounds and smell of a good firefight—after all, that's what we do best and get paid for!"

Primrose and Heto hunkered down near the edge of the airfield, looking into the thick jungle. "Heto, look just to the right, at about two o'clock. See the shadow?"

"Yeah, Primrose I see it. Shit, I'm better than anyone on the planet at this snooper stuff."

"Okay, okay, Heto. Jesus! I would like to point out that's the Jap we named Skoshi, the one we were telling you about. He follows us everywhere we go. To him, everyone at the old field is his enemy, and that includes our team and now you. He may be more directed towards the others, for he hasn't tried to engage us. I think he can see that we're fighting the same enemy he is. As you know, the Americans during WWII didn't have much of a presence in this area, so he doesn't know us from a hill of beans, but he can see who are going after."

"Primrose, I want to wait for the night and have Toms come along on the hunt, maybe between the two of us we can capture this Skoshi alive and talk him into bringing his cohorts in so we can send them all home."

"Sure, Heto, anything you say. The colonel should be back anytime. They've been gone a long while. I wonder what our orders will be? One thing for sure, we need to get on with it before they decide to fly the F-4s out of here with the weapons attached. I hope the colonel brings us good news, so we can get on with the program!"

Primrose heard Ourdae trying to be slick like an Indian and sneak up on him and Heto. "Ourdae, you just about got yourself killed. If you're going to sneak up on someone, you better get more in tune with the jungle and the good guys."

"Yes sir, I just crawled up here to tell you the colonel is back and is waiting at the dock. He wants you back there pronto. Toms told me to use a little Indian lingo."

"One word is not Indian lingo, Ourdae."

"It's the only one I could think of."

"Shit, you guys are hopeless. Heto, would you like to stay and keep an eye on Skoshi? I'll send Toms back to give you a hand."

"Sure, kemosabe."

"There you go, Ourdae, Heto know more Indian than you do."

"It's only one word, Lieutenant."

"True, Ourdae, but it's longer."

The longboat was heading back downriver, its operator happy to be shed of the Yankee warriors and to have a pocket full of their promissory notes.

The PT was rocking gently in the longboat's wake, but the tranquil scene wouldn't last long. The rubber was about to meet the road.

No one was in sight as Primrose came down to the dock, until O jumped up from the dinghy below the dock and yelled out, "The colonel is below decks, and he's really pumped. I think we're going to get this show on the road."

Primrose jumped down to the PT and reported in. "Lieutenant Primrose reporting as ordered, sir."

"Drop the bullshit and sit, Primrose, we've a lot of planning to do. The general, on recommendation of the carrier captain and the weapons officer, has decided we should recover the F-4s, weapons, and drivers, all intact and functional. They want everything back—leave nothing. And this is to be done at all costs."

"Sir, one thing before we get into how we're going to plan our attack and recovery. Heto is on the trail of Skoshi, and I've sent Toms to help him. Heto thinks they can capture him and talk him into helping them find the others and get them to surrender. If they can do that, the old soldiers may be able to help us; they would know things about the airfield that would take us days to learn. With that kind of information, it could be the edge we need to have a successful operation. As the colonel knows, we are few in numbers for the task at hand."

"You could be right, Primrose. I'll give them the rest of today and tonight, and if they can't get it done by then, we go ahead and make our move, come hell or high water! Lets go take another look at San Jose."

The colonel had that combat look in his eyes. His jaw was set in the manner of a prizefighter about to come out of his corner for round one in a championship bout. He was fully focused and ready for any situation that raised its ugly head. In a soft voice that belied his urgency, he said, "O, you and McPotts stay with the boat. Lieutenant, is Slipps still at the listening post?"

"Yes sir, he's been there all day. He's with Champion, who is salivating at the possibility of blowing one of the Genies. He thinks we should take one up to Hanoi and drop it on the SAM sites. He also wants to be the one to pull the trigger—his fantasy is to be within one foot of the bomb's radius, so he can watch it go and live to tell about it. And T.C. Champion is just one of the sick puppies you have in this motley crew."

"Okay, Lieutenant, Jesus. I didn't ask for a psychological profile, just his whereabouts. O, keep the PT warmed up and ready for a quick getaway. If you see us running down the dock, you know the drill. Martin, take the point; Ourdae, you stay in the middle with me. Lieutenant, you take Knight and bring up our six. Go Martin. Let's find Slipps."

Toms was mystified when he whispered to Heto, "Damn, Heto, how do you do that? You just appear out of fucking nowhere!"

Heto was not one to smile and show emotion, but he had to grin at that question. "You have to practice, Toms, and even then you'll never reach my level. You're a woods guy and I'm a jungle guy—big difference!"

Toms had to give it to Heto, he was the best he'd ever had the pleasure to work with. And that was hard to admit, coming from a tribe of tracker-hunters. Toms decided to study his every move and learn how the hell he could just disappear into the night whenever he wanted. He also hoped they could save the old Japanese soldiers and send them home.

"Heto, I'm out every night doing this shit, and I'm nowhere close to doing it like you do. There is more to this than practice. It's more like something the shamans can do: it seema almost mystical. I'll hound you until you show me *the way*. How close is Skoshi?"

"He's over there by the creek, just ahead. I think he's filling his canteen. We'll just follow him until he returns to his base camp."

Toms could see the tattered old soldier bending over in the water, his clothes torn and ragged; but when he stood up, his back was straight, his military bearing intact. After many long years of dedication to his country, he still looked capable of inflicting damage.

If they could find his base camp, they'd know how many other holdouts there were, and then Heto could try and convince them the war had ended in 1945, and they should give it up and go home. But capturing Skoshi alive might be a problem.

"There he goes, Toms, and he's not being very careful. I think he's been here so long that complacency has set in. He's making a lot of errors. I'll bet their base camp is not far from the tarmac. With the jungle so dense, it could be a hundred yards off the tarmac, and no one would know."

"Heto, you don't suppose he knows we're following him, and he's leading us into something?"

"That's a possibility—look, he's heading towards the airfield."

"Heto, there's the camp; he doesn't know we're following him, or he wouldn't have led us here."

"Oh shit, Toms, look behind you!"

"Fuck, I guess we underestimated him by a mile!"

Heto shouted back, not having to whisper any longer, "They have us dead to rights, our future is in their hands. Damn!"

The two super-trackers had just been snookered by a guy who should be half in the bag from so many years in the jungle.

"Heto, they have us completely surrounded and there are no happy faces."

Skoshi looked pretty good, compared to the rest of the old warriors. Their uniforms were barely recognizable. Only their peaked hats with the small bills looked intact and their rifles clean and menacing. The fact that they were still standing was a plus for the team. Toms remarked to Heto, "Its time to use some of that Japanese lingo, like right now, man! They're your brothers, get the fuck on with it!"

Heto, seeming to be in a place where calmness and tranquility abounded, said, "The big guy in front says for us to drop our weapons. Jesus, they're popping up all over the place. We'd better do whatever he says. If they were going to kill us, we'd already be dead. Damn, these guys are good!"

Toms dropped his rifle, pistol, knife and blow gun, as he retorted, "You told me you were the best, Heto."

Heto was not happy with the situation and like Toms, dropped his weapons. "I'm the best in my generation. Anyway, what difference does it make now? I guess we know how Custer felt at Little Big Horn when your people had him by the gonads."

Toms had to smile on that one, even though the situation was deadass serious, "Custer was trespassing and had it coming."

"Toms, put your hands on your head, and we'll follow that little prick just in front of us."

Toms could see the little guy over Heto's shoulder. There were at least twenty-five more surrounding them. Figuring some on guard duty and some out on roving patrols, that would make their force around fifty or so. "Heto, how did fifty of these guys survive so long in this shithole of a place?"

"Well, this must be the main camp. I can see Skoshi; he's standing by the camouflaged entrance to their HQ. They don't seem surprised or pissed. I really need to talk to their CO. Maybe we can get out of this with our scalps! With a little luck, we can get them to help us against a mutual enemy. They want you to wait here. Should I be a good Jap and have them string your ugly ass up in that tree over there?"

"Not funny, Heto. And the scalps shit was British, not Indian. Get on with some of the Japanese gibberish, we may be in some serious sheep-dip here!"

"I'll be out as soon as I can convince these guys the war is over, and they should surrender to us and turn over their weapons."

Toms had been standing among the old Japanese soldiers for an hour, wondering whether he'd be shot or hanged from the nearest tree, or just summarily beheaded with a Samurai sword, when Heto walked out of their HQ with the officers in tow and a big smile on his face. Toms didn't know whether they were letting Heto off the hook and and would only kill him, or whether Heto had been successful in his negotiations.

Heto raised his arm and pointed at Toms, then to the Japanese officer, who was holding his sword out to him. Toms shouted out, "What the fuck do you want me to do?"

"Take the sword. You are the representative of the United States Government. They're surrendering to you and will be your prisoners."

"How the hell did you do that?"

"I told them we were here to kill Russians, Chinese, and Koreans. That we're now allies against the others. I explained how the battle for my homeland of Okinawa, and the bombings of Nagasaki and Hiroshima brought an end to the war. I went on to explain that in the world today, Japan is a super economic power and allied with the United States. The commanding officer and his staff were in tears before I finished.

"While they were in tears, I convinced them not to kill you, even though you were the poster boy for the ugly American. Finally, I revealed our mission to recover the jets and told them what the jets were capable of. Their CO told me it was their duty to blow up the airfield and not let the enemy to utilize it. I replied that was fine—just let us get the jets up and away first—and we had a guy who had special talents with explosives and he would help them make the airfield disappear.

CHAPTER 17

The Alliance

McPotts was standing on the dock next to the PT, when three figures appeared out of the thick jungle. He yelled up to O, "You see what I see?"

O, who was standing on the bridge of the PT, replied, "I think so. It looks like Toms, Heto, and a Japanese army officer!"

"I believe you're right, O. If I know my military history, the guy is an army general from WWII. Damn!"

As the trio approached the dock, Toms said, "Gentlemen, you may salute the general. He may be our prisoner, but protocol suggests he's entitled to the respect of a salute."

McPotts stood and saluted the general and remarked, "Okay, Toms, lighten up; we could just as well have shot the three of you, not knowing who was leading who. You came close to being victims of friendly fire."

"Okay, McPotts, I get the point. Where's the colonel?"

"The colonel is having another look at the tarmac and buildings. He'll be back before dark. Where did you guys find the Nip general? He looks a little worse for wear."

Heto laughed at that one and remarked, "Don't let appearances fool you. He and his troops are very capable—they just snookered Toms and me, big time. They led us right into an ambush, but as you can see they didn't open up on us. We were outfoxed by a bunch of old soldiers who have been at war since the thirties."

As they watched the old general, they could see the relief in his eyes and the softness coming back to his face. The old guy must have thought he was going to end his days in this country and not go home to be given a proper burial, similar to how an old Indian chief would feel, being on a reservation and not going to a traditional hunting grounds for a suitable Indian burial. The general stood ramrod straight. He had to be at least seventy, with lots of gray, nearly white, hair.

"O."

"Yeah, Toms."

"How about taking the general below and giving him something to eat while Heto and I go find the colonel!"

"Ten-four."

General Fleetside was mired in an administrative nightmare. Being a grunt officer at heart, he wasn't pleased to oversee the present flap and its appearance of a convoluted mess, rather than the well-oiled machine going in the direction the general wanted.

"Sir."

"Yes, Captain Marks."

"Admiral Buckster is aboard."

"Thank you, Captain. Please show the admiral in."

The admiral was not one for a lot of conversation, and he had the look of a man on a mission as he stepped into the general's office. "General Fleetside, we've a major flap going on here. May we get right to the point?"

"Welcome aboard, Admiral. Would you care for a cup of coffee?"

"No, General. Let's get this flap over Admiral Dimflipper in perspective. The admiral has had a fine career, and the Navy wants it to stay that way. There are a couple of things you need to know about him. Aside from being a genius in naval tactics, the admiral is in a program wholly comprised of former POWs from the Korean War.

"This group has been closely monitored since their release from the camps. We've been eyeballing these people since the day they crossed the DMZ. As of today, the program has detected fifty who were programmed one way or another. Of the fifty, there are twenty who have never been contacted. Until now, the admiral was one of those twenty, which means we are down to nineteen. Our efforts to reverse the programming in their heads have failed.

"The admiral has been aware of the program since the beginning and until now hadn't been contacted. He is unaware of the orders given to the F-4 drivers and the weapons crew. Thanks to the very observant Marine corporal on duty with the admiral, we now know the trigger word being used. That means we can reverse the programming, which will allow the admiral to be his own man again. The burden he's carried for so many years will be removed.

"He'll be our first opportunity to reverse the damage in the former POWs. In the meantime, we don't want the enemy to know we know, so we're keeping the admiral aboard till the outcome of the jets is settled. If they try to make contact again, the admiral needs to be present for us to make our move, depending on what the contact says."

General Fleetside was getting a twitch in his neck. *Where had he heard of this Buckster before? If his memory served him correctly, Buckster was the de facto head of some high-dollar think tank, liberal group, led by his liberal bent. He was head of the research and development department, in addition to his position at the helm of the organization. Why Washington had sent him to watch this situation was a mystery. His forte was theoretical stuff, not the kind of live action going on here. In the past he'd had a tendency to let his mouth overload his candy-ass—he'd bear watching. Seems Murphy always has an admiral up a general's ass!*

"Admiral Buckster, we have a team in Cambodia as we speak, with orders to retrieve the F-4s, pilots, and weapons. From our limited information, it appears the Russians and Chinese paid big bucks, with future promises to the Koreans for the use of the admiral. The problem the team has is there are hundreds of those countries' troops in the area guarding the booty. We believe the reason they haven't tried to move the jets is because they wanted to wait until the search was called off, and they wouldn't be detected by our overflights.

"We need to keep the flyovers going, they'll think we're still hot and heavy in our search. They'll hunker down and wait for us to throw in the towel. The longer their heads are down, the better it'll be for our team on the ground. If all goes well, we'll have the birds, pilots, and weapons out sooner rather than later. There is one fly in the ointment, there are some old Japanese soldiers who haven't surrendered from WWII. The poor fellows don't believe the war has ended, and they're still defending the field. The colonel in command of the team requested a special agent from Okinawa to try and get them to give it up. The colonel will be reporting in before his team makes their move on the airfield, and he'll let us know the status of the Japanese soldiers at that time.

"Admiral Buckster, you say there are nineteen more of these sleepers that you know about. Are there any in this theater?"

"Of the remaining nineteen, there is one in this sphere of operations, yes, but I'm not at liberty to reveal his identity or whereabouts. We're close to him at all times, and he's under our control."

"Guess you guys kinda missed the boat on Admiral Dimflipper? A real fuckup, as I see it."

"You can't win them all, General. I'm heading back to the carrier to keep tabs on the admiral, and I would appreciate your cooperation on keeping this quiet—please keep me informed on your troops in Cambodia."

"Sure, no problem, you're first on my list." *What an arrogant prick, I don't think I'll be telling him shit!*

After the swelled-up asshole left the general's office he turned to Captain Marks. "Get Colonel Easy on the radio, landline, or whatever the fuck works!"

Captain Marks got right through on the radio and reported, "General, the colonel is in the bush and will be back at dusk. The radio guy on the PT boat said he'd get back to us the minute the colonel returned."

"Captain, keep the radio manned until we hear from the colonel."

"Yes sir."

Finding Slipps was not a problem, because he was where he was supposed to be, but if they had not known his position, they wouldn't have found him. His camouflage skills were second to none.

The colonel whistled to get Slipps's attention, and exposed his position so as not to test his shooting accuracy.

Slipps signaled his recognition of the colonel and Lieutenant Primrose.

After they crawled up to his position, the colonel asked Slipps, "Has anything unusual happened since you've been here?"

"Colonel, everything is the same. These dumb fucks think they're invisible. During the day they stay pretty much indoors or under the jungle canopy. At night they are out and about like cats in heat. Sir, I think we can take this field with the team we have now."

The colonel responded, "You might be right, Slipps. One colonel, a lieutenant, and a few good men may be all we need to finish this mission. Being the leader of this motley crew and wholly responsible for its outcome, I would like to call in a few IOUs, but that won't be possible, so we'll have to make do with a few good Marines and a couple of brown-water sailors. Martin, you and Knight stay here and report any changes. We'll return at dusk. When we meet the Marine pilot again, we'll have a clearer picture, and with all the shared intelligence a nice plan should present itself. Let's head back to the dock. Primrose, you lead out. Slipps, you bring up the rear. Everyone else fall in."

The hump back to the dock was getting easier each time, but they were leaving a trail a blind man could discover, but hopefully not before the team made their move on the airfield. The colonel was smiling as always in the bush, not even aware of his happy face. When they approached the dock, the PT looked the same, with O standing watch. A sneaky grin showed his white teeth, as he looked at the colonel.

"Okay, O, what's on your mind, and what's so fucking funny?"

"Sir, with all due respect, you are now outranked on the PT. We have a Japanese general on board!"

"You have what!"

"That's right, sir, a real live Jap brigadier general, a little the worse for wear, but nonetheless a general."

"All right, O, out with it. What's up?"

"Sir, Toms and Heto brought back a general from the airfield."

"No shit! Well, let's see the general, O. Bring him topside."

"Yes sir."

O yelled down below to Toms, "The colonel says to bring up the general."

"Belay that order," said the colonel. "Toms, you come topside and explain what the hell is going on."

Toms didn't get topside quick enough, so the colonel said again, "Toms, quit pissing around and get your ass up here!"

"Yes sir, I'm on my way."

As Toms appeared up through the hatch on deck, the colonel said, "Now tell me what the fuck O is talking about."

"Sir, to make a long story short, Heto and I got ourselves captured by the WWII holdouts. They snookered us clean as you please—they know the jungle here like the back of their hands after twenty or so years of tramping around here.

"Heto is really embarrassed, the great tracker from Okinawa getting sucked in by some forty-plus old men, all in his element. I have an excuse: I'm Indian tracker, woods are my domain, me not jungle man of his caliber, that's his playground."

"Toms, if you don't shut up with the rhetoric and get to the point, I'll personally have you hanged from the yardarm!"

"Yes sir. To make a long story short—"

"Toms, one more warning shot, and then it's curtains for you."

"Sir, Heto explained the world situation as it was in the forties and the world today. After an hour of questions and answers, they believed Heto and surrendered, and the general presented his sword to me. All the Jap POWs are back in their base camp, except for the general. The best part, sir, is the Japs are willing to help us capture the airfield. The best part, number two, is there are over fifty of them."

"What have you left out, Toms?"

"That's it sir. Heto will translate for you."

"Okay, bring the general topside."

Colonel Easy was thinking, *Damn, isn't it ironic that the last surrender of the Japanese Empire will not have taken place on the battleship Missouri? Accepting the final surrender of the Empire would be quite an honor for a lowly lieutenant colonel. There wouldn't be much of a crowd to witness the historic event; only those present would have something to tell their grandchildren.*

The general came up from below decks, freshly shaven, his tattered uniform squared away—what was left of it. His dignity intact, as he presented himself to the colonel and offered his sword, which Heto had returned to him after the encounter with Toms, saving it for the general to give to Colonel Easy in the best tradition of surrender.

The sword was pristine, gleaming with years of polish and care. This was the official surrender, from one commanding officer to another. The colonel saluted the general, and he returned a crisp salute of his own. When he handed Colonel Easy the sword, the colonel could see small tears forming in the old general's eyes. He stood ramrod straight at attention as he announced he was at the colonel's service.

Heto could feel the pain and relief in the old general as he translated, and the usual stern, stoic persona within him began to fade as the emotion of the general's surrender took center stage for all to see.

Colonel Easy broke the spell, "Heto."

"Yes, Colonel."

"Inform the general that he and his troops are now allies with the United States, that we are honored to have them on our team, and that we will provide transportation for their return to Japan as soon as the present situation is addressed.

"Let him know the reappearance of the general and his troops after almost twenty years will be worldwide news for weeks. That they will be heroes of the first order. Japan will finally put the war behind them, and a grateful nation will honor their sacrifice and dedication to duty."

The colonel went on to tell the old soldier they would be bombarded by the new media in print and on television. Heto translated that the general wanted to know what television was. Colonel Easy said, "Tell him he'll know soon enough, but there are more important matters at hand. Ask him, since he has defended the airfield for a number of years, what would be the best way for the newly formed alliance to capture the field intact?"

Heto, after explaining to the general what the colonel wanted, waited patiently for his reply and then translated. "The general says the armies now occupying the airfield are ignorant and cavalier. They'll be no problem. If the colonel has some tea, he would like to sit, enjoy the pleasure of a fresh cup, and discuss their options."

Colonel Easy replied, "Tea we can do. Ourdae, get some tea and fix it for the general and myself. Lieutenant, get everybody ready to head back to the tarmac. We should be ready to attack tonight or at first light.

Toms, you and Knight get going right now. We'll meet you near the outbuilding by the hangar. The F-4 driver can climb back out and give us the bottom line on the birds. See you then! Primrose, you sit in on the powwow. Heto, tell the old general we need to move on the airfield tonight, or at least by dawn."

The old general took his seat below decks and sipped his tea in a manner befitting royalty. He was obviously pleased to have a fresh cup of honest-to-goodness tea. His smile was uncommon for his stature. The Japanese soldier, sticking to the Bushido Code, were not known for exposing their feelings. Nearly twenty years in the jungle may have tempered the general just a bit.

"Colonel, the general says he was ready twenty years ago. If we concentrate on the outbuildings and hangars, he and his troops will take care of the rest. He doesn't want to be responsible for the aircraft."

"Wise man, that general. Living in the jungle for so many years hasn't dulled his political savvy. Tell him to work out the details with Lieutenant Primrose while I talk to our CO and bring him up to date. O, get General Fleetside on the horn. We need to hit the ground running!"

CHAPTER 18

Final Preparations

"Colonel."

"Yes, O."

"General Fleetside is on the air."

Colonel Easy picked up the handset. "Colonel Easy here, General. We're using the radio because of time restraints."

"Get on with it, Colonel."

"Yes sir. Sir, all we have left to do is contact the Marine pilot one more time, and then we make our move. One other thing, General, we've acquired fifty Japanese soldiers. They are now our allies in the battle to come. They surrendered to us wholesale. It is quite a story, sir."

General Fleetside remarked, "Colonel, do not share any more of your fantasies with me. Just tell me what you need for the mission."

"Sir, if we had a Chinook, we could pick up the lame bird with missiles intact and carry it out of here. The other bird is flyable. We aren't equipped to carry the Genies by hand."

"Colonel, there are two Chinooks at a B-52 base in Thailand. I'll dispatch one to the embassy in Phnom Penh, along with a couple of gunships for escort."

"Thank you sir, we'll direct the chopper from the embassy to our position up river."

"Anything else, Colonel?"

"No sir."

"Get to it, Colonel."

"Aye, aye sir. Sir, there is one more thing to consider. The matter of the Japanese holdouts; we could use the other Chinook to carry them out. There are close to fifty—after the battle maybe less."

"Okay, Colonel, you get two Chinooks and two gunships."

"Thank you, sir. I'll keep in touch."

"Good hunting, Colonel."

The Japanese general was excited about doing battle with the Koreans, Russians, and Chinese, all his sworn enemies. He said his troops were ready and could have their part of the battle secure within an hour or so, under the present conditions. His troops were in place and eager. They decided on a green flare at daylight to get the attack underway. The daylight attack would give them more time in the dark of night to snoop around and have another chat with the Marine fighter pilot.

Colonel Easy was anxious and asked Primrose, "Lieutenant, have you and our newfound allies gotten your battle plan in order?"

"Yes sir."

"Okay then; let's get back to the airfield. You and Slipps lead out. I'll take the middle with Champion. Martin, you cover our six with McPotts. Heto, you take one of the radios and the general and head for his troops.

"Keep in constant contact. Do not allow him to be more than one foot from you. We can't afford to be without his troops. Let's keep him healthy so he and his people can return home intact, with dignity and honor.

"We'll hump it to the hangar area and hook up with Toms and Knight. Our next move will be to have a chat with the Marine wing wiper. We'll send him back with a couple of Colt .45s to give us some inside assistance. Once they take out their guards, a couple of AK-47s will be available for additional firepower."

"Colonel."

"Yes, Heto."

"The general and I will be on our way. He knows a shorter way to his troops. He and I agree it'll be a pleasure to dump on these Commie assholes. He wishes you luck and that this will be he and his troops' last hurrah. He says it will be a relief to finally end the war with a taste of combat after so many years. His Bushido Code will be intact and fulfilled in spades."

The colonel saluted the general as they disappeared into the thick foliage.

"O."

"Yes sir."

"You and Ourdae stay with the PT and keep the channels open. If anything comes your way, we need to know what you're up to. My radio sign will be Umpire; the PT will be Home Plate; Primrose will be Pitcher and Heto, Catcher. Let's move out!"

The outbuildings were barely visible, just shadows in the darkness. Primrose almost ran into the building. Toms and Knight had a lot of fun watching him almost fuck things up. They sprang out of the tall grass and scared the shit out of everybody.

Knight was having a great time being away from his typewriter and learning from the night owl Toms. They all gathered around the colonel for the attack orders.

"Gentlemen, it's time for all of our experience and training to come into play. Martin, you, Champion, and I will go around to the right side of the hangar. Primrose, you take Knight, Toms, and Slipps around to the outbuilding where the pilots are. Let's do it!"

When they had slipped around to the pilots' temporary quarters, Primrose told Toms, "Get your ass down to the hoosegow and get the Marine captain back here pronto. He sent Slipps to the left of the hangar, to look for any new security and to be sure things were as before inside.

Knight and Primrose could see Toms in the dim light from the hoosegow throwing pebbles at the shack's window. "Where the hell did he find pebbles in this green quagmire?" remarked Knight. Finally the window slid to one side and the captain climbed out, only to fall headfirst out of the opening. Toms was able to break his fall, keeping him from injuring himself and fucking up the flight out. Being quiet was not the forte of a fighter jockey.

They could hear Toms chewing the captain's ass. It was pretty funny considering their rank difference.

After some confusion, they crawled back to the jungle apron. As they got closer, Primrose whispered, "Hello, Captain. We're about to get the show on the road. Our attack will begin at dawn."

The captain was stoked to the brim, thinking he was leaving the shack for good, but was disappointed when Primrose continued, "I've got a couple of Colt .45s for you. Our mission is to capture the airfield, bring in a Chinook to take out the wounded bird, and get you two airborne with the other bird. You'll find your way back to Yankee Station and the *Hornet*."

The Marine captain, not happy with the return to the shack, said, "Lieutenant, I'm not a pessimist, but from what I gather, there can't be more than ten of you! How many of the enemy—one, two hundred?"

"Yes, there are at least a hundred, probably double that, but with the help of some old Japanese soldiers and with surprise on our side, we'll prevail. Don't forget, we're Marines and odds don't mean much in our business—we're very good at what we do. Now take the pistols and do a number on your guards, they'll not be expecting any challenges from inside.

"When you hear the shit hit the fan from outside, your guards will be distracted for a moment and that's your signal to take them out. When the shooting stops, stay put until you hear from us. We need you and Navy in flying condition. No one else can take your place. So stay out of the line of fire until we come for you. If all goes well, the field will be in our control within an hour and you guys can get the hell out of Dodge!"

Primrose and Knight could see the captain and Toms crawling back to the temporary brig, and they could make out the Marine captain standing on Toms' shoulders as he climbed back through the window. When Toms returned, he was mumbling something about how loud the captain was, and had considered cutting he captain's throat if he made any more noise.

About the time the Marine captain hit the floor in the shack, they could hear Umpire report they were ready. Champion answered, "We're in position, the pilots are armed."

Heto checked in, "Land of the Rising Sun is in position for the assault."

And Murphy, if he followed his history, would be standing by, willing to rain on their parade! As the teams were settling in waiting for the dawn, a call came in from Home Plate. "There are scores of radio traffic on the river, could be someone is monitoring our airwaves. You might watch out for an alert at the field. We're heading downriver to a slough that is not far off and take on any latercomers."

The colonel stepped in, "Belay that, Home Plate. This is Umpire. Head upriver. If they put in a call for assistance, it'll come there. I'm sending McPotts back to give you a hand, wait for him."

"Ten-four."

"Umpire, this is Pitcher, there is activity here, looks like the bad guys feel something is up, but they don't know what!"

"Umpire, this is Catcher, same here, they're stirring."

"This is Umpire. Listen up, they don't know who, how, or where, so just sit tight, be cool, and use your best judgment."

"Umpire, this is Pitcher, they've sent out a few guards to check things out, but no patrols, so we can handle it."

The colonel responded, "Stay focused, gentlemen."

After all the chatter settled down, the colonel got back on the radio, "Home Plate, report when McPotts is aboard, and you're heading upriver."

It was near daylight when Home Plate called. "Sir, we have company coming down the river. They're still a ways off, but coming fast, we can hear them more than see them. It's about thirty minutes before light, but we'll engage and begin to hammer them at three hundred yards. Oh, by the way, McPotts would like to thank the colonel for having the good sense to put his swabby ass back on the PT, where he belongs. He was going to quit the Marines after this mission and rejoin the Navy, with the colonel's permission of course!"

"Home Plate, keep in touch. We may need your river taxi at any moment. If things go bad here, we'll be heading for the dock on the double."

CHAPTER 19

The Final Campaign

As the colonel and Primrose waited for the dawn, they could hear the battle raging on the river, both from the radio and from the sound bleeding through the predawn mist. Primrose remarked to the colonel, "Jesus, they must really be in the shit!"

The distinct sound of the twin fifties blasting away could only mean the bad guys were getting a pasting. The thumping of mortar rounds could be heard, but they didn't know whose was whose.

Colonel Easy said, "Those three rogues can handle it. I believe they could hold off Alexander the Great with the firepower on the boat and their brown-water experience. The gunfight can have only one outcome; victory for the PT."

"Umpire, this is Home Plate. As you can probably hear, we have engaged the bad guys. We have them stalled, they can't get by us, but how long we can hold them is questionable. We've plenty of ammo, but are outgunned by three boats to one. Ourdae and McPotts are hit, but not serious. Our best weapon is that we can out-maneuver them. The choppers have arrived at the embassy. McPotts gave them the coordinates to the dock and airfield. Our engagement is giving a whole new meaning to close order combat. If we get any closer, boarding parties will be needed, and if I recall my history, boarding was the forte of the Old Corps. Thank God we shoot better than they do!"

After the brief report from the PT, the colonel yelled out to Primrose, "Let loose the flare!" Thump went the green flare, sending up the signal for the attack to commence. The old Japanese soldiers from the former empire of WWII were about to engage in their last battle, before going home to a hero's welcome.

Toms took down the guard nearest him, as Knight dropped the guard next to the shack's door. Surprise was on their side, the guards never had a chance. The pilots chipped in right on cue. They could hear lots of shooting inside; they hoped the pilots were winning.

The whole airfield was now alerted and firing wildly into the jungle, but the bad guys couldn't see much in the dim light and thick foliage. Toms and Knight were shooting from the front side of the shack, picking them off like ducks in a shooting gallery, plunk, plunk. Slipps crawled up to the back side of the shack to give the pilots a hand. Surprise or not, they had the enemy totally confused.

The colonel yelled over to Martin, "Do you see the asshole behind the tree over there?"

"Yes sir."

"When he sticks his head out again, hit him."

"No need to wait, sir."

The colonel watched as Martin slowly squeezed the trigger, and the next thing he saw was the Korean falling flat on his kisser from behind the tree, drilled in the head through the trunk—he never knew what hit him.

Champion was spraying the guards around the hangar with the M-60, aiming low so the rounds wouldn't penetrate the hangar skin and hit the F-4s. Colonel Easy jumped out of the jungle and attacked the front of the hangar. He looked like the mad hatter crossed with the Cheshire cat, grinning from ear to ear as he cut the bad guys down like bowling pins.

The battle was one-sided, big time. The enemy wasn't prepared for such an onslaught by a few good men. The old Japanese general had been right: the defenders were slackers. Colonel Easy had really fucked up their day!

Heto radioed in to report they had control of both ends of the tarmac, and were walking it to clear all the debris.

Colonel Easy answered, "We're at the front of the F-4 hangar and ready to clear it. It won't be long before the F-4 will be on its way. Be sure there are no objects in its way!"

Martin had cleared the rear, while Slipps had opened the door to the outbuildings to discover the pilots had won their battle with the guards inside. The two were shaken but ready to climb into the flyable jet and get the hell out of Dodge. Slipps let the colonel know that the Navy driver had a hip wound, but it wasn't debilitating—he could fly.

Toms, Knight and Primrose ran around to the back to help Martin, who had been hit. His leg had a nice hole, and there was a crease down the middle of his head, which was bleeding like a stuck pig.

"Umpire, this is Catcher, all secure on our end."

"Umpire, this is Pitcher, all secure from the outbuildings and hangars."

"Primrose, I'm standing right in front of the F-4s, you don't have to yell into the radio!"

"Yes sir, didn't see you there, glad you weren't one of the bad guys."

"Where are your people, Primrose?"

"Sir, they're outside, setting up a defensive position, and the pilots are just behind the hangar doors."

"Have the pilots come in and check out the F-4s for damage. No fucking around, Lieutenant, we don't have a lot of time."

The radio kept chattering. "Umpire, this is Home Plate, we can't hold out much longer."

"Home Plate, start retreating and make your way back to the dock."

"Ten-four sir, we'll be there with the posse on our ass, unless the Marines show up to save the day!"

"Umpire, this is Chinook One, we have visual."

"Chinook One, head for the largest hangar, the F-4s are in there. Do you have gunships with you?"

"Ten-four."

"Chinook One, send the gunships upriver to help a WWII PT boat heading downriver with three gunboats on their stern. Have the gunships hit the attacking boats. Our guys will have green smoke coming from their bows."

"Ten-four, Umpire."

"Home Plate, did you read that transmission?"

"Roger that, Umpire, thanks. I guess the Marines will show up after all to save the brown-water sailors."

Colonel Easy continued on the radio, "Catcher, have you finished walking the tarmac for trash? The F-4 will be taking off posthaste."

"Roger, Umpire."

Colonel Easy turned to the Marine captain, "Get the bird ready for takeoff. The choppers are on the way in. We need to hurry this up. We don't know what else they have to throw at us. Does the tow vehicle work?"

"Yes sir, it did when we landed."

"I'll have Primrose bring it in. You jump in the cockpit and get things started."

Not wanting to be left out, the Navy pilot said, "Colonel, if you can get someone to help me climb into the lame bird, I will do my part here and steer it out for the Chinook to pick up."

"Okay, Navy. When Lieutenant Primrose gets back with the tow vehicle, we'll hook up and get you guys out of here. Champion, help the Navy into the cockpit."

The radio was popping in and out with everyone getting into the act. "Chinook One, this is Umpire, touch down on the south side of the hangar; Chinook Two, go to the north side. Chinook One, are you equipped for the F-4 pickup?"

"Ten-four, Umpire, ready for trash haul."

The Navy pilot heard the reference to trash haul, and yelled down to the colonel. "Tell that chopper pilot we'll have a discussion about that remark when we get back to friendly hands."

The colonel relayed the Navy comment to the chopper.

As the colonel was relaying all the radio chatter, a round coming from the jungle passed by his head. "Jesus, what the hell was that, Primrose?"

"Colonel, I think we have a sniper winging at us."

Primrose yelled out to Champion, "Find Martin, and tell him we have a sniper, opposite the hangar from the tarmac."

"Yes sir, Lieutenant."

Another round slammed into the cockpit bubble. "Damn, there he goes again. Boy, that was close. You okay, Navy?" asked the colonel.

"Yes sir, but it was a close one."

"Come on, Primrose, get the bird hooked up and out of here, the chopper is waiting," yelled Easy.

"Yes sir, and thank God, the good F-4 is taking off and heading for feet wet and the *Hornet.* Sir, his radio doesn't work. Those Russian clowns tried to rig the radios for their frequency and they fucked them up. Same with this one."

"Shit, there he goes again! That's the third shot, he may have missed but he's getting closer. Where the hell are Martin and Toms?" roared the colonel.

Primrose answered, "Sir, Martin and Toms are hot on his trail. It shouldn't be long."

"Toms, did you see the flash that time?"

"Yeah, he's about 1500 yards up the tarmac on the south side near that old piece of equipment."

"Okay, listen Toms, do some of that Indian shit and draw his fire!"

"Fuck you, Martin. I know he's a bad shot, but he might get lucky at my expense. You do some of that white man's shit!"

"Whoops, there he goes again, Toms!"

"What's the matter now, Martin? Jesus, you can't quit whining for a minute."

"That son of a bitch hit my bayonet."

Toms retorted, "Damn! I told you he might get lucky. Quit sniveling, Martin, he could have hit your grenades, you dumbass. If the sucker moves just an inch, he's mine. There he goes—whack, right in the melon."

"Just in time, Toms, the F-4 just lifted off."

Back at the hangar, the colonel was directing fire and ordered Primrose, "Tow out the F-4. It's time."

"Yes sir, on the way."

Easy keyed the radio, "Chinook One, we're pulling the injured bird out now."

"Ten-four, we're ready for extraction—Colonel, we're taking some incoming."

"Sorry about that, Chinook, our guys have taken out the sniper.

"Chinook Two, stay put until One is away. We have forty or so troops to pick up. Keep your door gunners alert, we don't know what the enemy has left. Your troop pickup will be some old Japanese soldiers left over from WWII. That may sound way out there, but it's true."

"Sure, Colonel, we buy that, and your private jet back to the real world is on standby."

"Umpire, this is Home Plate, we're near the dock; thanks for the additional firepower. Those gunships did a number on the gunboats. Score three for the home team and zip for the visitors. We don't know whose boats they were, but whoever, their Navy is three short of a load. Where did you find the First Cav in this part ofthe world?"

"Home Plate, when you reach the dock, report in and keep the engines running and ready for a boarding party, we may be in for a quick trip downriver. The First Cav was in Phnom Penh on a diplomatic mission, and they were the closest choppers available. I think Schroud had something to do with their convenient location and timing."

"Umpire, this is save-your-ass choppers A & B. We heard through the grapevine about some action in this area, and we needed some excitement, so we headed this way. You guys do get around, and with your reputation we could count on you having your ass in the fire. Hope you have an additional request, so we can hang out till you say skedaddle. Schroud out."

The colonel asked Schroud to hang by for a while longer; they might need additional firepower down the road.

The good bird was in the air, and the broken bird was ready for extraction.

About the time they were ready to hook up the injured F-4, they got a call from Catcher that they were under fire from some bad guys who got past them. Catcher reported the enemy was heading towards the hangar area. Before the colonel could relay the message, the sound of automatic weapons rang out. They hit the deck and returned fire across the tarmac into the thick jungle foliage.

The chopper had to go back around to the side of the hangar, but not before it was raked with a barrage.

The colonel got on the radio to Schroud, "This is Umpire, please engage troops attacking hangar—we can't see them."

"We see them, right on, Umpire, we knew we could count on you for additional adventure. We're on them like white on rice."

Primrose reported to the colonel, "Sir, the Chinook won't be able to pick up the F-4. Their rigging was shot away and the other chopper doesn't have that capability. We can still use the choppers to pick up the Japanese soldiers."

Easy responded, "Soon as the gunships eliminate the present threat, we'll take care of the remaining F-4."

"Yes sir."

"Hell, Primrose, get Champion and Slipps over here, we need to offload the Genie rockets now and blow the F-4! Shit, all we need now is to be carrying around a fucking nuke rocket by hand. We should have sent the Navy driver out with the other F-4. Get the bird back into the hangar, before they hit the rockets. Damn!"

"Slipps."

"Yes, Lieutenant."

"Can you get the rockets off and loaded on the tow vehicle? We need to get them out to the chopper. The F-4 can't be lifted out of here, so we'll put the Genies on the chopper for a ride back to civilization."

"No problem, Lieutenant, just need a few more hands. The Genies weigh about 800 pounds. We need to drop them straight down onto the tow vehicle, then I can drive right up to the chopper. Piece of cake."

Primrose turned to Champion, "Start thinking about how you're going to destroy the F-4, I mean everything, nothing left-period."

"Yes sir, Lieutenant, can do. Like Slipps said, piece of cake."

The colonel called Heto, "When will you have your sector under control?"

Heto replied, "With First Cav helping out, it won't be long."

The colonel then checked with Home Plate, "What's your status?"

McPotts answered, "Colonel, we're back at the dock licking our wounds. We are ready, willing, and able to continue thanks to Doc Ourdae—the guy is a wizard."

"McPotts, we'll be heading for the dock in less than an hour."

"Colonel, the river is free of bad guys for now, but we won't take bets on the near future!"

"Hang in there, we won't be long," replied the colonel.

"Well, Slipps, what the fuck is the hang-up?

"Sir, we don't need to take these Genies off."

"Slipps, this is no time to be shitting around, get the damned things off, now!"

"Sir, these Genies are ATR-2s, dummy rounds. The kind used for practice firings. They look the same from the outside, but inside—nothing but weights! I'm wondering if the other two are also dummies."

"You mean to tell me all this shit we've been through may have been for fucking dummy nukes?"

"Yes sir, these are blanks. I don't know about the others. We can't get the Marine driver on the radio. As you know his radio is out of action, and he probably wouldn't know if they were live or not anyway."

Colonel Easy called out for Champion. "Champion, blow the bird, hangars, and anything else you find interesting."

"Yes sir, for a sick puppy like me, that's the best order I've ever heard. It'll be my pleasure to make dust out of this airfield, along with lots of fire—and it doesn't hurt to have some earth-shattering noise as well."

The colonel got Heto on the radio and told him to get his Japanese forces over to the hangar as soon as they mopped up the remaining enemy combatants. With the gunfight won, they could board the choppers for their final journey home.

After Heto, he notified Home Plate to stand by; the team would be on their way shortly.

Schroud radioed the enemy had been eliminated and they were out of fuel and ammo, so they were heading for the barn, but to keep in touch if another mission came up.

The colonel asked, "Does your general know you're in Cambodia supporting Marines?"

"Sir, we heard about your not-so-secret operation and put two and two together. We manipulated some paper work and people, which landed us on a diplomatic taxi job. Piece of cake as they say. See ya, and thanks!"

"Primrose, get the troops together. We're heading for the dock as soon as we get the Nips loaded and on their way. Champion will pull the trigger when we're out of range."

CHAPTER 20

Mission Accomplished

"Sir."

"Yes, Primrose."

"I couldn't figure why the admiral used the F-4s for his ruse; but now I know. He needed to have a two-seated jet. It was the only way to have two empty seats to pick up the supposed POW pilots. Saying the jets were equipped with all the high tech stuff was just a cover story, so no one would take a second look."

"Sounds good to me Lieutenant, maybe we can ask the admiral when he gets his head clear of all the Commie muck."

"Thanks, Colonel, I would like to ask the admiral to confirm a few things."

When it looked like everything was falling into place, and they could get the hell out of Dodge, Murphy raised his ugly head.

Martin reported he'd lost contact with Toms, so the colonel decided to wait for Heto to catch up and then Heto would help Martin. It was unlike Toms to get separated from anyone or anything he didn't want to, so they had to figure something was definitely out of whack.

While they were waiting for Heto, the colonel asked Champion, "How is the HE going?"

"Sir, it's going to be a beautiful thing, with multi-colored fire and brimstone. I've thrown in a bunch of C-4 and a few additions of my own concoction. It'll be magnificent, sir."

"Champion, this is no time to be dicking around, there are people left out there who want a piece of our ass—now get on with it!"

"Sir, sometimes I think you don't see the beauty of things."

"Get on with it, Champion. I am capable of shooting you!"

"Yes sir, I'll be ready shortly. You know sir, I don't understand why people don't stop and smell the burning powder or enjoy the flash-bang!"

"You're a sick puppy Champion. You should seek counseling when we get back to friendly skies."

"Thank you, sir. I'll think about that for a second or so."

Heto and his WWII troops arrived at the hangar with heads high and a smart step in their march on the tarmac. The colonel saluted the general and asked him to divide his troops between the two choppers, to begin their journey home. Heto told the colonel there was a small problem. The soldiers had five dead from the battle to secure the tarmac, and they wouldn't leave them behind. The colonel replied, "Damn, Heto, what are we going to do with five dead bodies?"

"Colonel, they won't go without them, and as I recall, the Marines don't leave anyone behind either—that's the Marine way, right?"

"Okay, okay, Heto, you've made your point. When you have them aboard, get with Martin. Toms is missing, and you need to go help find his Indian ass."

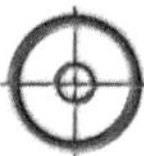

"Umpire, this is Chinook One, where do we drop our passengers?"

"Chinook One and Two, take them to the American Embassy in Phnom Penh. I'll call ahead to let them know your ETA. Thanks for the help: we owe you—beach party on us!"

Heto was off with Martin looking for Toms, so the colonel told Primrose to help Champion finish setting the charges and then go assist in the search for Toms. He and the others would head for the dock and hopefully, be far away when Champion pulled the trigger on his HE cocktail.

The colonel wanted to get back to the dock, so he could call Rhonda and have her get with Cleo and alert the two embassies about the arrival of the old Japanese soldiers, and then call HQ and inform the CG of the recent events and present situation.

"Step it up, gentlemen, we don't have much time. The choppers will be at the embassies before we can contact them. Their arrival without notice would throw them into shock."

After the resident pyrotechnic genius finished, they hurried off to help find Toms. As they got farther and farther away from the hangar, Primrose kept expecting Champion to blow the place. He finally said, "Well? When are you going to let it loose?"

Champion, retorted, "We're not far enough away yet!"

While they were heading into the jungle, Primrose asked Champion, "How the hell could Toms get lost? This whole area is no bigger than a piss ant. He has roamed all over Vietnam and Laos in the fucking dark, without losing his way. He must be down—shit!"

"You see him, Martin?"

"Yeah, Heto. He's tied up and bleeding from the neck and head. There are five or six bodies laying around him and three live guys guarding him. Looks like he's out cold or playing possum—either way, it must have been some fight."

"Martin, I'll circle around and make sure we are alone with the present cast of characters."

"Go ahead. I'll hang here and make sure these three mind their manners. Heto, these fuckers look Chinese. What do you think?"

"Not sure, could be from eastern Russia. Anyway, who cares? When we're sure the area is clear, they are going to die and meet their maker."

"Lieutenant, get ready—the airfield is about to go. Maybe we should find something to get behind. This will be a whopper!"

The words had just left Champion's lips when the sound of the explosion rattled the jungle. The ground shook, the sky went black, and the thunderous noise was just the prelude: the shock wave that hit them rivaled a full load of bombs dropped from a B-52 at close range.

"Jesus Christ, Champion, what the hell was in that load, to get that frigging shock wave?"

"It was just a little cocktail I made from all the available material. Isn't it beautiful? Just look at all the shit flying overhead, and the sound is incredible!"

"I've got to hand it to you, Champion, that was one hell of a job. I'll bet there's nothing left but a grease spot!"

"There is no doubt about that, Lieutenant Primrose. I'm the best there is—hands down."

"I'll vote for that. Let's find Martin and Heto."

O yelled out over the thunder of the shock wave, "Damn, Colonel, it sounds like Champion just blew one of the nukes. You don't suppose he fucked up, and one of those Genies was the real thing? Look at that smoke and debris falling all the way to the river. The shock wave could have created a tsunami!"

"Ten-four, O. I agree that Champion is one sick fuck. Now get Rhonda on the radio. After we fill her and Cleo in on the present situation, we'll update Division."

"Sir, I have Rhonda now."

"Rhonda, no time for explanations. Please get hold of Cleo and pass on the situation to her. Heto managed to negotiate a surrender with the Japanese soldiers, and they are on their way to the embassy. You might keep things quiet until you notify the Japanese Embassy, and then let them carry the ball from there. I told the Japanese general we'd fly them home, so see about getting a C-130 if the Japanese Embassy can't provide transportation. Let me know how it plays out, we'll keep in touch."

"Ten-four, thank you. Talk later, Colonel."

Colonel Easy turned to O, "Get the general at Division on the horn."

McPotts and O had the PT ready to head down-river as soon as Heto, Martin, Toms, Champion, and Primrose showed up.

The assholes at the airfield they'd just dumped on might have a few surprises left in their bag. They had to be more than a little pissed about losing the Genies and the F-4s. In addition, the Koreans would have to return all the money and goods they had traded. There is a great pissing contest going on! The Russians are pissed, the Koreans are pissed, and the Chinese too.

As they waited for the other troops, Colonel Easy was thinking, *If I find out the other two rockets are also dummies—someone will have a royal ass-kicking coming. After all we've been through, the others better be real. I hope the mission hadn't been planned to cover up for some jerk-off or to keep it under wraps that our side knew about the admiral. I could lose my commission for choking some bureaucrat to death.*

"Colonel."

"Yeah, O."

"The commanding general is at the Officers Club. Division is patching you through."

The general's voice came through loud and clear. "Lieutenant Colonel Easy, tell me what I want to hear."

"Sir, one of the F-4s is on the way home if he's not there already. He was to give you a belly roll before going feet wet and the *Hornet.* The second F-4 was broken beyond all repair. Champion, our resident explosive expert, blew the jet, dummy Genies, the hangars, and all the buildings—the airfield is dust.

"We decimated the enemy forces with few, if any, survivors. We didn't stick around for a head count. The Navy driver is with us, and we'll be coming down-river in the PT. The Japanese troops are heading for the American Embassy, and we're waiting on one missing trooper before we shove off."

"Colonel, did I hear you say dummy Genies? Did I hear you correctly?"

"Yes sir, the Genies on the broken bird were prac-tice dummies. I don't know about the others. Slipps didn't get to look at them. When the bird took off, we were in the middle of one heavy-duty-firefight. Sir, I have some serious reservations about this mission. We had a lot at stake for some dummy rockets."

"Colonel, stand by; I'll get the ship's captain and weapons officer on the other line."

"Yes sir, that was my next suggestion."

Primrose was crawling in the thick brush towards a clearing, when he heard a familiar voice, "Quiet, Lieutenant, you want to give us away?"

"Damn, Martin! You scared the shit out of me. What the hell is going on here? Where's Heto?"

Primrose could see Toms in the clearing. He looked unconscious—or dead. He whispered to Martin, "What do you think?"

"Lieutenant, I think he's playing possum, and he might have enough talent for a second career after returning home."

The three men looking over Toms seemed nervous and ready to make a move into the jungle after killing Toms if he wasn't already dead.

"There's Heto now, Lieutenant. If those are the only ones left, we'll take them down and get Toms off the hook, one way or another."

"How's it look, Heto?"

"It's all clear all around: what we see is it. Can't figure what they're waiting for. They have to know what's taken place, with the explosion and the battle for the airfield over. Either of those two events should have been their clue to disappear and fight another day."

"Martin, you take the one on the left. I'll get the center guy. Heto, you take out the right side. I'll count to three, and—bingo! Let's do it."

"Wait a minute, Lieutenant. Maybe we should see if they want to surrender?"

"Slipps, if they thought for a minute we were here, Toms would be dead. Besides, we don't have time for any negotiations, nor are we equipped to take care of prisoners".

"Sir."

"Jesus, what now?"

"What about me? I do all the heavy shit with the HE, and now I have a chance to be a real grunt and you leave me out."

"Damn, Champion, we don't have time to draw straws."

"Sir, how about I take them on? I sneak around and jump them from the other side as you distract them from here."

"No way, Champion, they might cut Toms throat before you got them all. Maybe next time we can find a one-on-one for you.

"On my count, one, two, three—bingo! Good job. Home team three, visitors zip!"

With the three enemy soldiers dead to the world, Toms made a sudden recovery and jumped up yelling, "It took you fuckers long enough to get your sweet asses here. Shit, you take a taxi or what? I could've crawled here quicker. These guys were getting real shaky about doing me in and getting the hell out of Dodge!"

Primrose remarked, "Would you mind shutting your mouth, Toms? You look like shit. What the hell happened to you? I'm beginning to think the great American Indian hunter is losing his touch."

"Lieutenant, you won't believe what happened!"

"I know Toms, but tell me anyway. Was it something like you saw a vision and came this way to find your sniper?"

"No sir, I came this way chasing one of those fucks—and I don't chase, I hunt. There is a difference. But in the heat of battle, I lost a little self-control, not my style. This asshole had really pissed me off, and he led me right into one of those old tiger pits. This one shitbird played me like a violin and led me right to it, but it was old and not very deep. I was just climbing out when I looked up, and there stood the three stooges. They motioned me out of the pit and took me over to this clearing, where the rest of the happy group were hiding. By the sound of the language, I figured right then they were going to kill me. So I thought, *What the hell, they're not getting me for free.* I jumped and threw a cross-body block on the nearest guy that had an AK-47. I knocked him down and recovered the weapon. I got a short burst off and took out four right in front of me, but the damned thing jammed, so I pulled out my trusty Ka-Bar and got two more before the three stooges bagged me from behind. Why they didn't kill me right away was a mystery, until I heard the word hostage slip from their conversation. I was gonna be their insurance policy for freedom if they got caught by good guys.

"But as the day wore on, they were getting itchy feet, and I think they were going to just shoot me and take their chances in the jungle.

"You could have planned things a little better and gotten here sooner. I supposed you dragged your feet so you could watch Champion pull the trigger on the airfield fireworks? The explosion and shock wave scared the shit out of these three. Other than that, I've had a nice day."

"Are you finished, Toms?"

"Yes sir."

"Colonel, the general is back on the two-way."

"Thanks, O."

General Fleetside was beside himself as he addressed Colonel Easy, "Colonel, I have talked with the carrier captain and his weapons crew. This is how it shakes out. The captain was in the dark about the whole mission, and he's one very irritated son of a bitch. He can't put two words together, he's so fucking pissed, and I don't blame him. I feel sorry for the crew and anyone else who even blinks without permission. Personally, I would've strung the weapons officer and his crew from the yard-arm, put the admiral under house arrest, brought the carrier about, and headed into the wind, bound for Subic Bay, where I would have proceeded with a general court martial for the lot of them.

"But that's not to be the case. As we know, the admiral was not responsible because of the POW thing. The weapons officer didn't know for sure about the admiral, but had his suspicions after talking with the same Marine that you spoke with. The weapons officer decided to make only half a mistake.

"We're lucky the dummy rockets happened to be on the broken bird. The mission was not in vain, Colonel Easy. Now, what's your status?"

"General, Champion destroyed the broken bird, hangars, and all the other buildings at the old Japanese field. During the attack we eliminated most of the competition. Not many, if any, survived the battle. We loaded the old soldiers into the Chinook, and you should be getting a call from the U. S., and Japanese embassies, announcing the arrival of the last Imperial Troops.

"The Japanese general was in tears, praising his troops for nearly twenty years of devotion to duty and country. Their fighting spirit in the last battle proved to be in the highest tradition of the Bushido. As each soldier boarded the chopper, he turned in my direction, saluted, bowed, and handed over his weapons. They're bringing five of their dead from the last battle home with them. They will receive a hero's welcome.

"Sir, I still have some stragglers to pick up, and as soon as they show, we'll board the PT and head for Phnom Penh, Bangkok, and then to Division."

"Colonel, you and your troops have done an out-standing job. I believe there will be some personal decorations for the lot of you. I might add that just because you got lucky on this mission, it doesn't mean I've forgotten the last few times you've had my ass in a sling. The checkbook isn't balanced—you still owe me!"

"Yes sir, I'll pass that along to my people."

Colonel Easy could see the general grinning and wishing he'd been in the field from the get-go.

"Colonel, here come the lost stragglers, and it looks like Toms is in bad shape."

"Okay, Ourdae, get down there and fix him up. Jesus, that's what you get paid for."

"Yes sir. On my way."

Primrose could see the colonel counting heads, a stern look on his face that didn't show the concern he had for his troops. He was shaking hands with each one as they boarded the PT. There were four wounded, but nothing serious.

Primrose was happy, and the troops were in good spirits, coming off the high of combat—a hard thing to top!

The combat high was what kept them coming back again and again. It's the excitement of not knowing what's around the corner, of testing one's training and skills, of pitting oneself against the enemy. Fighting for freedom has always been, and always will be, a good thing.

Primrose was looking forward to a couple of weeks in Bangkok with Rhonda. The colonel wanted to get to know Cleo better, and the troops wanted to get back to the routine of their regular duties—if there ever was such a thing.

Primrose would bet the farm there would be another request for them to perform the impossible!

"There are only two kinds of people who understand Marines: Marines and the enemy. Everyone else has a second hand opinion."
General W. Thorson, U.S. Army

ABOUT THE AUTHOR

R. Michael Haigwood is a Marine Veteran, life member and past Commandant of the Black Mountain Detachment, Marine Corps League, and a member of the Black Mountain Harley Davidson Owners Group (HOG). He has been a big hole driller, underground diamond driller, heavy equipment operator, hotel bartender, bellhop, blackjack dealer, union negotiator, and Senior Olympics athlete. He is a longtime resident of Las Vegas, Nevada, where he lives with his partner, Jean.

GLOSSARY

0141	USMC Military Occupational Specialty Code (MOS) for administrative clerk in the Vietnam era
Arty	Artillery
Bird colonel	A colonel with a pay grade of O-6, rather than O-5. A higher-ranking colonel than a lieutenant colonel.
CG	The Commanding General
CID	Criminal Investigation Division
Corpsman	Any enlisted United States Navy medical personnel ("Doc") who treats United States Marines in the field
Cover	A military hat
CP	Command Post
CWO-4	Marine gunners are non-technical Chief Warrant Officers (CWO-2 to CWO-5) who are weapons specialists knowledgeable in the tactical employment of all infantry weapons in the arsenal.
Deadlined	Refers to equipment down for maintenance or repairs
Driver	A military aircraft operator, e.g., an F-16 pilot is called a "Viper driver."
EM Enlisted	Men's club
Fast mover	Military jet
Feet dry (or wet)	When an airplane moves over land or water
First shirt	First sergeant
FO post	Forward observation post
Grease gun	An M3 .45 caliber submachine gun
Hat Out	Slang for leave (a place)

212

Have Someone's Six....The phrase originated with World War I fighter pilots referencing the rear of an airplane as the six o'clock position. "Bringing up your six" means "I've got you covered, so the enemy can't come up behind you." "I've got your back."

HE..................................High Explosive

LRRP.............................Long Range Reconnaissance Patrol

LSD...............................(Landing Ship, Dock) An amphibious ship with a well dock to transport and launch landing craft

LZ ....Landing zone

MCRD...........................Marine Corps Recruit Depot

MCSC...........................Marine Corps Supply Center

NVA..............................North Vietnamese Army

OP ....Observation post

PBR...............................Patrol Boat, Riverine

Piss-cutter.....................A foldable military cap, e.g., an FMF piss-cutter, (Fleet Marine Force overseas cap)

Puff the Magic Dragon...Dragonships, the AC-47 gunship, with its broadside battery of GE miniguns, spewed a stream of red phosphorus tracers.

Q Clearance..................Clearance to access top secret restricted data

Rack..............................Bed

Six-by............................The 6X6 heavy duty cargo truck used by the Marines during the Vietnam War

SRB...............................Service Record Book

The Rock......................Okinawa

The Sweet Science.......Boxing

Top...............................First Sergeant

UDT ....Underwater Demolition Team

Ville..............................A small village or group of huts

Wing wiper...................Any member of the U.S.M.C. Air Wing